Aphra Behn

The Feign'd Curtizans

A nights intrigue. A comedy. As it is acted at the Dukes theatre. Written by

Mrs. A. Behn

Aphra Behn

The Feign'd Curtizans
A nights intrigue. A comedy. As it is acted at the Dukes theatre. Written by Mrs. A. Behn

ISBN/EAN: 9783337780654

Printed in Europe, USA, Canada, Australia, Japan

Cover: Foto ©Andreas Hilbeck / pixelio.de

More available books at **www.hansebooks.com**

THE
Feign'd Curtizans,
OR,
A Nights Intrigue.
A
COMEDY.

As it is Acted at the
Dukes Theatre.

Written by Mrs. *A. BEHN.*

Licensed *Mar.* 27. 1679. *ROGER L'ESTRANGE.*

LONDON,
Printed for *Jacob Tonson* at the *Judges Head*
in *Chancery-Lane* near *Fleet-street.* 1679.

T O
Mrs. *ELLEN GUIN.*

Madam,

TIS no wonder th:t hitherto I followed not the good example of the believing Poets, fince lefs faith and zeal then yon alone can infpire, had wanted power to have reduc't me to the true worfhip : Your permiffion, *Madam*, has inlightened me, and I with fhame look back on my paft Ignorance, which fuffered me not to pay an Adoration long fince, where there was fo very much due, yet even now though fecure in my opinion, I make this Sacrifice with infinite fear and trembling, well knowing that fo Excellent and perfect a Creature as your felf differs only from the Divine powers in this ; the Offerings made to you ought to be worthy of you, whilft they accept the will alone ; and how Madam, would your Altars be loaded, if like heaven you gave permiffion to all that had a will and defire to approach 'em, who now at diftance can only wifh and admire, which all mankinde agree to do ; as if Madam, you alone had the pattent from heaven to ingrofs all hearts ; and even thofe diftant flaves whom you conquer with your fame, pay an equall tribute to thofe that have the blefling of being wounded by your Eyes, and boaft the happinefs of be-

A 2

holding

holding you dayly ; infomuch that fucceeding ages
who fhall with joy furvey your Hiftory fhall Envy
us who lived in this, and faw thofe charming wonders which they can only reade of, and whom we
ought in charity to pity, fince all the Pictures, pens
or pencills can draw, will give give 'em but a faint
Idea of what we have the honour to fee in fuch ab-
folute Perfection ; they can only guefs She was infinitely fair, witty, and deferving, but to what Vaft
degrees in all, they can only Judge who liv'd to
Gaze and Liften ; for befides Madam, all the
Charms and attractions and powers of your Sex, you
have Beauties peculiar to your felf, an eternal fweet-
nefs, youth and ayr, which never dwelt in any face
but yours, of which not one unimitable Grace could
be ever borrow'd, or affumed, though with never
fo much induftry, to adorn another, they cannot
fteal a look or fmile from you to inhance their own
beauties price, but all the world will know it yours ;
fo Natural and fo fitted are all your Charms and Excellencies to one another, fo intirely defign'd and
created to make up in you alone the moft perfect
lovely thing in the world; you never appear but you
glad the hearts of all that have the happy fortune to
fee you, as if you were made on purpofe to put the
whole world into good Humour, whenever you
look abroad, and when you fpeak, men crowd to
liften with that awfull reverence as to Holy Oracles
or Divine Prophefies, and bears away the precious
words to tell at home to all the attentive family,
the Gracefull things you utter'd and cry, *but oh fhe*
fpoke.

spoke with such an Ayr, so gay, that half the beau-ty's lost in the repetition. 'Tis this that ought to make your Sex vain enough to despise the malicious world that will allow a woman no wit, and bless our selves for living in an Age that can produce so wondrous an argument as your undeniable self, to shame those boasting talkers who are Judges of no-thing but faults.

But how much in vain Madam, I endeavour to tell you the sence of all mankinde with mine, since to the utmost Limits of the Universe your mighty Conquests are made known : And who can doubt the Power of that Illustrious Beauty, the Charms of that tongue, and the greatness of that minde, who has subdu'd the most powerfull and Glorious Mo-narch of the world : And so well you bear the ho-nours your were born for, with a greatness so unaf-fected, an affabillity so easie, an Humor so soft, so far from Pride or Vanity, that the most Envious & most disaffected can finde no cause or reason to wish you less, Nor can Heaven give you more, who has exprest a particular care of you every way, and above all in bestowing on the world and you, two noble Bran-ches, who have all the greatness and sweetness of their Royal and beautiful stock; and who give us too a hopeful Prospect of what their future Braveries will perform, when they shall shoot up and spread themselves to that degree, that all the lesser world may finde repose beneath their shades ; and whom you have permitted to wear those glorious Titles which you your self Generously neglected, well

knowing

knowing with the noble Poet ; 'tis better far to me-
rit Titles then to wear 'em.

Can you then blame my Ambition, Madam, that
lays this at your feet, and begs a Sanctuary where all
pay so great a Veneration ? 'twas Dedicated yours
before it had a being, and overbusy to render it
worthy of the Honour, made it less grateful ; and Po-
etry like Lovers often fares the worse by taking too
much pains to please ; but under so Gracious an In-
fluence my tender Lawrells may thrive, till they become fit Wreaths to offer to the Rays that improve
their Growth : which Madam, I humbly implore,
you still permit her ever to do, who is,

Madam,

Your most humble,

and Most Obedient Servant.

A. Behn.

The

The PROLOGUE,
Spoken by Mrs. *Currer*.

THE devil take this cursed plotting Age,
'T has ruin'd all our Plots upon the Stage ;
Suspicions, New Elections, Jealousies,
Fresh Informations, New discoveries,
Do so employ the busie fearful Town,
Our honest calling here is useless grown ;
Each fool turns Politician now, and wears
A formal face, and talks of State-affairs ;
Makes Acts, Decrees, and a new Modell draws
For regulation both of Church and Laws ;
Tires out his empty noddle to invent
What rule and method's best in government ;
But Wit as if 'twere Jesuiticall,
Is an abomination to ye all :
To what a wretched pass will poor Plays come,
This must be damn'd, the Plot is laid in Rome ;
      'Tis hard——yet——
Not one amongst ye all I'le undertake,
Ere thought that we should suffer for Religions sake :
Who wou'd have thought that wou'd have been th'occasion,
Of any contest in our hopefull Nation ?
For my own principles, faith, let me tell ye
I'me still of the Religion of my Cully,
And till these dangerous times they'd none to fix on,
But now are something in meer contradiction,
And piously pretend, these are not days,
For keeping Mistresses and seeing Plays.
Who says this Age a Reformation wants,
When Betty Currer's Lovers all turn Saints ?
In vain alas I flatter, swear, and vow,
You'l scarce do any thing for Charity now :
Yet I am handsome still, still young and mad ;
Can wheadle, lie, dissemble, jilt——egad,
As well and artfully as ere I did,
Yet not one Conquest can I gain or hope,
No Prentice, not a Foreman of a Shop,
So that I want extremely New Supplies ;
Of my last Coxcomb, faith, these were the Prize ;

And by the tatter'd Enſignes you may know,
Theſe ſpoils were of a Victory long ago :
Who wou'd have thought ſuch helliſh times to've ſeen,
When I ſhou'd be neglected at eighteen ?
That Youth and Beauty ſhou'd be quite undone,
A Pox upon the Whore of Babylon.

The Actors Names.

Italians.

Mr' *Norris.*	*Moriſini.*	An Old Count Uncle to *Julio.*
Mr. *Crosby.*	*Julio.*	HIs Nephew, a young Count, con-tracted to *Laura Lucretia.*
Mr. *Gilloe.*	*Octavio.*	A young Count contracted to *Marcella,*-deform'd, revengeful.
	Crapine.	*Moriſini*'s man.
Mr. *Liegh.*	*Petro.*	Suppos'd Pimp to the two Cur-tezans.

Engliſh.

Mr. *Smith.*	Sir *Harry Fillamour.*	In love with *Marcella.*
Mr. *Betterton.*	Mr. *Galliard.*	In love with *Cornelia.*
Mr. *Nokes.*	Sir *Signall Buffoon.*	A fool.
Mr. *Underhill.*	Mr. *Ticklerext,*	His Governour.
	Jack. Sir *Signals* man.	

Women.

Mrs *Lee.*	*Laura Lucretia.*	A young Lady of Quallity, contract-ed to *Julio,* in love with *Galliard,* and Siſter to *Octavio.*
Mrs *Currer.*	*Marcella.* and	Siſters to *Julio,* and Nieces to *Mo-riſini,* paſs for Curtizans by the
Mrs *Barry.*	*Cornelia.*	Names of *Euphemia* & *Silvianetta*
Mrs *Norris.*	*Phillipa,*	Their Woman.
Mrs *Seymour.*	*Sabina,*	Confident to *Laura Lucretia.*

Pages, Muſick, Footmen, and Bravo's.

SCENE, *Rome.*

THE

Feign'dCurtizans,

OR,

A NIGHTS INTRIGUE.

ACT I. SCENE I.

Enter Laura, Lucretia, *and* Silvio *richly dreſt* ; Antonio *attending, Coming all in in haſte.*

Silvio.

MAdam, you need not make ſuch haſte away, the Stranger that follow'd us from St. *Peters* Church, purſues us no longer , and we have now loſt ſight of him : Lord who wou'd have thought the approach of a handſome Cavalier ſhould have poſſeſt *Dona Laura Lucretia* with fear ?

Lau. I do not fear my *Silvio,* but I wou'd have this new Habitation which I've deſign'd for love, known to none but him to whom I've de-ſtin'd my heatt : ——ah wou'd he know the Conqueſt he has made, [*Aſide.*] Nor went I this evening to Church with any other Devotion, but that which warms my heart for my young Engliſh Cavalier, whom I hop't to have ſeen there, and I muſt finde ſome way to let him know my paſſion which is too high for ſouls like mine to hide.

Silv. Madam, the Cavalier's in view again, and hot in the purſuit

Lau. Lets haſte away then, and *Silvio* do you lag behinde, 'twill give him an opportunity of Enquiring, whilſt I get out of ſight,——be ſure you conceal my Name and Quality, and tell him——any thing but truth——tell him I am *La Silvianetta* the young Roman Curtizan, or what you pleaſe to hide me from his knowledge.   [*Exeunt* Lau.

Enter Julio *and Page in Purſuit.*

Jul. Boy fall you into diſcourſe with that Page, and learn his Ladys Name——whilſt I purſue her farther.   [*Exeunt* Jul.

Page ſalutes *Silvio,* who returns it, they go out as talking to each other.

B   *Enter*

Enter Sr Harry Fillamour *and* Galliard.

Fill. He follows her clofe, whoe're they be : I fee this trade of Love goes forward ftill.

Gall. And will whilft there's difference in Sexes. But *Harry* the wo-men, the delicate Women I was fpeaking of?

Fill. Prethee tell me no more of thy fine Women, *Frank*, thou haft not been in *Rome* above a Month, and thou'aft been a Dozen times in Love as thou call'ft it : to me there is no pleafure like Conftancie.

Gall. Conftancy ! and woudft thou have me one of thofe dull Lovers who believe it their Duty to Love a Woman till her Hair and Eyes change Colour for fear of the Scandalous Name of an inconftant ! No, my Paffion like great Victors hates the lazy ftay, but having vanquifht, prepares for new Conquefts.

Fill. Which you gain as they do Towns by Fire, lofe 'em even in the taking, thou wo't grow Penitent and weary of thefe Dangerous follys.

Gall. But I am yet two young for both : Let old Age and infirmity bring Repentance, ——there's her feeble Province, and even then too we finde no Plague like being depriv'd of dear Woman-kinde.

Fill. I hate Playing about a Flame that will confume me.

Gall. Away with your Antiquated Notions, and let's once hear fence from thee : Examine but the whole World *Harry*, and thou wilt finde a Beautifull woman the defire of the Nobleft, and the reward of the Braveft.

Fill. And the common Prize of Coxcombs : times are alter'd now, *Frank,* why elfe fhou'd the Virtuous be cornuted, the Coward be careft, the Villain role with Six, and the Fool lye with her Ladyfhip.

Gall. Meer Accident Sir : and the kindnefs of Fortune, but a Pretty witty young Creature, fuch as this *Silvianetta,* and *Euphemia,* is cer-tainly the greateft blefling this wicked World can afford us.

Fill. I believe the Lawful enjoyment of fuch a Woman, and honeft too, wou'd be a blefling.

Gall. Lawful enjoyment ! Prethee what's lawful enjoyment, but to enjoy'em according to the generous indulgent Law of Nature ; en-joy'em as we do Meat, Drink, Ayr and Light, and all the reft of her common blefings ;---therefore prithee dear Knight, let me govern thee but for a day, and I will fhew thee fuch a *Signiora,* fuch a Beauty, an-other manner of piece then your fo admired *Vitterboan, Dona Marcella,* of whom you boaft fo much.

Fill. And yet this rare piece is but a Curtizan, in courfe plain Eng-lifh, a very Whore !——

Who filthily expofes all her Beautys to him can give her moft, not Love her beft.

Gall.

Gall. Whe faith, to thy comfort be it fpoken, fhe does diftribute her charms at that eafy rate.

Fill. Oh the vaft diftance between an innocent paffion, and a poor faithlefs Luft.

Gall. Innocent Paffion at *Rome*! Oh 'tis not to be nam'd but in fome Northern Climat: to be an Anchoret here, is to be an Epicure in *Greenland*; impoffibillities *Harry*! ——

—— Sure thou haft been advifing with Sir *Signal Buffoons* Governor! that formall piece of nonfenfe and Hipocrifie.

Fill. No faith, I brought the Humour along with me to *Rome*, and for your Governor I have not feen him yet, though he lodge in this fame Houfe with us, and you promis'd to bring me acquainted with long fince.

Gall. I'le do't this very minute!

Fill. No, I'me oblig'd not to engage my felf this Evening, becaufe I expect the arrival of Count *Julio*, whofe laft Letters affur'd me wou'd be to night.

Gall. *Julio*! What the young Itallian Count you made me acquainted with laft Summer in *England*?

Fill. The fame, the Ambafadors Nephew; a good youth and one I efteem.

Enter Julio.

Jul. I hope my Page will bring intelligence who this beauty is.

Fill. Hah, *Julio*! Welcome dear Friend.   [*Embraces him.*

Jul. Sir *Harry Fillamour*! how glad am I to meet you in a Country where I have power to repay you all thofe Friendfhips I receiv'd when I was a ftranger to yours.

Monfieur *Galliard* too, nay then I'me fure to want no diverfion whilft I ftay in *Rome*.   [*Salutes* Galliard.

Fill. But pray, what made you leave *England* fo foon?

Jul. E'ne the great bufinefs of Mankinde, Matrimony, I have an Uncle here who has provided me Fetters which I mnft put on, he fays, they will be eafy, I lik't the Character of my Miftrefs well enough, a brave Mafculine Lady, a Roman of Quality, *Dona Laura Lucretia*, till as luck wou'd have it at my arrival this Evening, ftepping into S. *Peters* Church, I faw a woman there that fir'd my heart, and whom I follow'd to her houfe; but meeting none that cou'd inform me who fhe was, I left my Page to make the difcovery, whilft I with equal impatience came to look out you; whofe fight I prefer even to a new Amour, refolving not to vifit home, to which I have been a ftranger this feven years, till I had kift your hands, and gain'd your promife to accompany me to *Vitterbo*.

Fill. *Vitterbo*! is that your place of Refidence?

Jul. Yes; 'tis a pretty Town, and many noble Familys inhabit there, ftor'd too with Beauties, at leaft, 'twas wont to be: have you not feen it?

B 2   *Gall.*

Gall. Yes! and a Beauty there too lately for his repofe, who has made him figh and look fo like an Afs ever fince he came to *Rome.*

Jul. I'me glad you have fo powerfull an argument to invite you back, I know fhe muft be rare, and of quality that cou'd engage your heart.

Fill. She's both, it moft unluckily fell out, that I was recommended by a Perfon of Quality in *England* to a Nobleman at *Vitterbo,* who being a man of a temper frank and gallant, receiv'd me with lefs Ceremony then is ufual in *Italy.* I had the freedom of the Houfe, one of the fineft *Villa*'s belonging to *Vitterbo,* and the pleafure to fee and converfe at a diftance, with one of the lovelieft perfons in the World, a Neece of this old Counts.

Jul. Very well, and cou'd you fee her but at diftance, Sir ?

Fill. Oh, no, 'twas all I durft defire, or fhe durft give ; I came too late to hope ; fhe being before promis'd in Marriage to a more happy man, the Confummation of which waits only the arival of a Brother of hers, who is now at the Court of *France,* and every day expected.

Enter Petro *like a Barber.*

Gall. Hah! Signior *Petro :*

Fill. Come Sir, we'l take a turn in the i'th gallery, for this pimp never appears but *Frances* defires to be in private.

Gall. Thou wrong'ft an honeft ingenious fellow to call him pimp.

Pet. Ah Signior, what his worfhip pleafes !

Gall. That thou art I'le be fworn, or what any mans worfhip pleafes, for let me tell ye *Harry,* he is capacitated to oblige in any quality ; for Sir, he's your brokering Jew, your Fencing, Dancing and Civillity-Mafter, your Linguift, your Antiquary, your Bravo, your Pathick, your Whore, your Pimp, and a thoufand more Excellencies he has to fupply the neceffities of the wanting ftranger.——Well firrah—— What defigne now upon Sir *Signal* and his wife Governor ;——What do you reprefent now ?

Pet. A Barber Sir.

Gall. And why a Barber, good Signior *Petro ?*

Pet. Oh Sir, the fooner to take the heights of their judgments, it gives handfome opportunities to commend their faces, for if they are pleafed with flattery, the certain fign of a fool's to be moft tickled when moft commended, I conclude 'em the fitter for my purpofe ; they already put great confidence in me, will have no Mafters but of my recommending, all which I fupply my felf, by the help of my feveral difguifes ; by which and my induftry, I doubt not but to pick up a good honeft painfull livelihood, by cheating thefe two Reverend Coxcombs.

Gall. How the Devil got'ft thou this credit with 'em ?

Pet. Oh eafily Sir, as knaves get eftates, or fools employments.

Fill. I hope amongft all your good qualities you forgot not your more natural one of pimping.

Pet.

Pet. No, I aſſure you Sir, I have told Sir *Signal Buffoon* ; that no Man lives here without his Inamorata, which very word has ſo fir'd him, that he's reſolv'd to have an *Inamorata*, whatever it coſt him, and as in all things elſe I have in that too promis'd my aſſiſtance.

Gall. If you aſſiſt him no better then you have done me he may ſtay long enough for his Inamorato.

Pet. Why faith Sir, I lye at my young Lady night and day, but ſhe is ſo loath to part with that ſame Maiden-head of hers yet——but to morrow night Sir ther's hopes.——

Gall. To morrow night ! Oh 'tis an Age in Love ! deſire knows no time but the preſent, 'tis now I wiſh, and now I wou'd enjoy, a new day ought to bring a new deſire.

Pet. Alas Sir I'me but an humble Bravo.

Gall. Yes thou'rt a pimp, yet want'ſt the art to procure a longing lover the woman he adores, tho' but a common Curtizan——Oh confound her Maidenhead——She underſtands her trade too well to have that badge of Innocence.

Pet. I offered her her price Sir——

Gall. Double it, give any thing, for that's the beſt receipt I ever found to ſoften womens hearts.

Pet. Well Sir, ſhe will be this Evening in the Garden of *Medoes Villa,* there you may get an opportunity to advance your intereſt—— I muſt ſtep and trim Mr. *Tickletext,* and then am at your ſervice !

[*Exit* Petro.

Jul. What is this Knight and his Governor who have the bleſſed fortune to be manag'd by this Squire ?

Fill. Certain fools *Galliard* makes uſe on when he has a minde to laugh : and whom I never thought worth a viſit ſince I came to *Rome* : and he's like to profit much by his Travells, who keeps company with all the Engliſh, eſpecially the Fops.

Gall. Faith Sir, I came not abroad to return with the formallity of a Judge ; and theſe are ſuch anditotes againſt Melancholy as wou'd make thee fond of fooling.——Our Knights Father is even the firſt Gentleman of his Houſe, a fellow, who having the good Fortune to be much a fool and knave, had the attendant bleſſing of getting an Eſtate of ſome eight thouſand a year, with this Coxcomb to inherit it ; who (to agrandize the Name and Family of the *Buffoons*) was made a Knight, but to refine throughout and make a compleat Fop, was ſent abroad under the Government of one Mr. *Tickletext* his zealous Fathers Chaplain, as errant a block-head as a man wou'd wiſh to hear Preach : the Father wiſely foreſeeing the eminent danger that young Travellers are in of being perverted to Popery.

Jul. 'Twas well conſider'd.

Gall. But for the young Spark there is no deſcription can reach him ; 'tis only to be done by himſelf ; let it ſuffice 'tis a pert, ſawcy, conceited

ceited Animal, whom you fhall juft now go fee, and admire, for he lodges in the houfe with us.

Jul. With all my heart, I never long'd more for a new acquaintance.

Fill. And in all probability fhall fooner defire to be rid on't. aloone.—— [*Exeunt.*

SCENE II.

Draws off, and difcovers Mr. Tickletext *a Trimming, his hair under a Cap, a cloath before him, and* Petro *Snaps his fingers, takes away the Bafon, and goes to wiping his face.*

Tickletext *and* Petro.

Pet. Ah che Bella! Bella! I fwear by thefe fparkling Eyes, and thefe foft Plump dimpl'd cheeks, there's not a Signiora in all *Rome*, cou'd fhe behold 'em, were able to ftand their Temptations, and for *La Silvianetta*, my life on't fhe's your own.

Tick. Teze, teze, fpeak foftly!——but honeft *Barberacho*, do I, do I indeed look plump, and young, and frefh and——hah!

Pet. Ay Sir, as the Rofie Morn, young, as old Time in his Infancie, and plump as the Pale-fac't Moon.

Tick. He——Whe this Travelling muft needs improve a Man,—— Whe how admirably well fpoken your very Barbers are here, ——[*Afide.*]——but *Barberacho*, did the young Gentlewoman fay fhe lik't me? did fhe Rogue? did fhe?

Pet. A doated on you Signior, doated on you.

Tick. Whe, and that's ftrange now, in the Autumn of my Age too, when Nature began to be impertinent, as a man may fay, that a young Lady fhou'd fall in love with me————[*Afide.*——— Whe *Barberacho*, I do not conceive any great matter of Sin only in vifiting a Lady that loves a man, hah.

Pet. Sin Sir, 'tis a frequent thing now adays in Perfons of your Complexion.

Tick. Efpecially here at *Rome* too, where 'tis no Scandal.

Pet. Ay Signior, where the Ladys are *Priviledg'd,* and *Fornication Licenc't.*

Tick. Right! and when 'tis Licens'd 'tis Lawful, and when 'tis Lawful it can be no Sin: befides *Barberacho*, I may chance to turn her, who knows!

Pet. Turn her Signior, Alafs any way, which way you pleafe.

Tick. He he he! There thou wert knavifh, I doubt——but I mean Convert her——Nothing elfe I profefs *Barberacho*.

Pet. True Signior, true, fhe's a Lady of an eafy Nature, and an Indifferent Argument well handled will do't——ha—— [*combing out his Hair.* here's your head of Hair——here's your Natural Frize! And fuch an Ayr it gives the Face!——So Signior——Now you have the utmoft my Art can do. [*takes away the cloth and bows.*

Tick.

Tick. Well Signior :——and where's your looking-glaſs.

Pet. My looking-glaſs.

Tick. Yes Signior your Looking-glaſs ! an Engliſh Barber wou'd as ſoon have forgotten to have ſnapt his fingers, made his leg, or taken his Money, as have neglected his looking-glaſs.

Pet. Aye Signior, in your Countrey the Laiety have ſo little ho-neſty, they are not to be truſted with the taking off your Beard unleſs you ſee't done,——but heres a Glaſs, Sir,   [*gives him the Glaſs.*

    [*Tick. Sets himſelf and ſmirks in the Glaſs,* Pet. *ſtanding behinde*
      him, making horns and grimaces, which Tick. *ſees in the Glaſs,*
      gravely riſes, turns towards Petro.

Tick. Whe how now, *Barberacho,* what Monſtrous faces are you making there ?

Pet. Ah my Belly, my Belly, Signior: ah, this Wind-Collick ! this *Hypocondriack* does ſo torment me ! ah——

Tick. Alaſs poor Knave ; *certo,* I thought thou hadſt been ſome-what uncivil with me, I profeſs I did ;

Pet. Who I Sir, uncivil ?——I abuſe my Patrone ?——I that have al-moſt made my ſelf a Pimp to ſerve you ?

Tick. Teze teze, honeſt *Barberacho* ! no, no, no, all's well, all's well :——but hark y'.——you will be diſcreet and ſecret in this buſineſs now, and above all things conceal the knowledge of this Gentlewoman from Sir *Signall* and Mr. *Galliard.*

Pet. The Rack Signior, the Rack ſhall not extort it.

Tick. Hold thy hand——there's ſomewhat for thee,   [*gives him* but ſhall I Rogue——ſhall I ſee her to night ?—— ——   *money.*

Pet. To night Sir, meet me in the Piatza *D'hiſpagnia,* about 10 a Clock,——I'le meet you there,——but 'tis fit Signior——that I ſhould provide a Collation,——'tis the Cuſtom here Sir.——

Tick. Well, well, what will it come to,——here's an Angel——

Pet. Whe Sir 'twill come to——about——for you wou'd do't han-ſomely——ſome twenty Crowns.——

Tick. How man, twenty Crowns ?

Pet. Ay Signior, thereabouts.

Tick. Twenty Crowns——Whe 'tis a Sum, a Portion, a Revenue.

Pet. Alaſs Signior, 'tis nothing with her,——ſhe'le look it out in an hour,——ah ſuch an Eye ! ſo ſparkling, with an Amorous twire——thus Sir——then ſhe'le kiſs it out in a moment,——ſuch a Lip, ſo red, ſo round, and ſo plump, ſo ſoft, and ſo——

Tick. Why has ſhe, has ſhe, Sirrah——hah——here, here, prethee take Money, here, and make no words on't——go, go your way, go—— but to entertain Sir *Signall* with other matter, pray ſend his Maſters to him ; if thou canſt help him to Maſters, and me to Miſtreſſes, thou ſhalt be the good Genius of us both : but ſee where he comes.——

                                                            Sir

Enter Sir Signall.

Sir *Sig.* Hah! *Signior Illuſtriſſimo Barberacho,* let me hugg thee my little *Miphiſtophiloucho*——de yee ſee here, how fine your Brokering Jew has made me, Segnior *Rabbi Manaſeth--Ben—Nebiton,* and ſo forth ; hah——View me round——   [*turns round.*

Tick. I profeſs 'tis as fit as if it had been made for you.

Sir *Sig.* Made for me——Whe Sir, he ſwore to me by the old Law, that 'twas never worn but once, and that but by one high-German Prince——I have forgot his name——for the Devil can never remember theſe damn'd *Hogan-Mogan* Titles.   [*a fart.*

Tick. No matter, Sir.

Sir *Sig.* Ay, but I ſhou'd be loth to be in any mans clothes, were he never ſo high a German-Prince, except *I* knew his name tho.

Tick. Sir, I hold his Name unneceſſary to be remembred, ſo long as 'twas a Princely penniworth.——*Barberacho* get you gone, and ſend the Maſters.   [*Ex.* Petro.

Sir *Sig.* Why how now Governour ! how now Signior *Tickletext* ! prethee how cam'ſt thou ſo tranſmografi'd, ha ? whe thou look'ſt like any new-fledg'd *Cupid.*

Tick. Do I, away you flatter, D⸜ *I* ?

Sir *Sig.* As I hope to breathe, your face ſhines through your powder'd hairs like you know what on a barn-door, in a froſty morning.

Tick. What a filthy compariſon's there for a man of my coat.

Sir *Sig.* What, angry——*Corpo di me,* I meant no harm,——Come, ſhall's to a *Bonaroba,* where thou ſhalt part with thy puſilage, and that of thy beard together.

Tick. How mean you Sir, a Curtizan, and a Romiſh Curtizan ?

Sir *Sig.* Now my Tuter's up, ha ha ha,——and ever is when one names a whore ; be pacifi'd man, be pacifi'd, *I* know thou hat'ſt 'em worſe then beads or holy-water.

Tick. Away you are ſuch another Knight——but leave this Naughty diſcourſe, and prepare for your Fencing and Civility-Maſters, who are coming,

Sir *Sig.* Ay, when Governour, when ; oh how I long for my Civility-Maſter, that I may learn to out-complement all the dull Knights and Squires in *Kent,* with a *Servitore Hulichimo*——*No ſigniora Belliſſima, baſe le Mane, de vos ſigniora ſcuſa mia Illuſtriſſimo, caſpeto de Bacco,* and ſo I'le run on, hah Governor, hah ! won't this be pure ?

Tick. Notably Ingenious, I profeſs !

Sir *Sig.* Well I'le ſend my *Staffiera* for him *incontinente.*——he, *Jack*—— a——*Cazo,* what a Damn'd Engliſh name is *Jack?* let me ſee——I will call him——*Giovanni,* which is as much as to ſay *John* !——he *Giovanni.*   [*Enter* Jack.

Tick. Sir, by your favour his Engliſh Proteſtant-Name is *John Pepper* ; and I'le call him by ne're a Popiſh name in Chriſtiandom.

                                                        Sir *Sig.*

Sir Sig. I'le call my own man Sir, by what name I pleafe Sir ; and let me tell you Reverend Mr. *Tickletext*, I fcorn to be ferv'd by any man who's name has not an *Acho*, or an *Oucho*, or fome *Italliano* at the end on't——therefore *Giovanni Peperacho* is the name by which you fhall be diftinguifht and dignify'd hereafter.

Tick. Sir *Signall*, Sir *Signall*, let me tell you, that to call a man out of his name is unwarantable, for *Peter* is call'd *Peter*, and *John*, *John*, and I'le not fee the poor fellow wrong'd of his name for nere a *Giovanni* in *Rome*.

Sir Sig. Sir I tell you that one Itallian Name is worth any two Englifh names in *Europe*, and I'le be judg'd by my Civility-Mafter.

Tick. Who fhall end the difpute, if he be of my Opinion.

Sir Sig Multo vollentiero, which is as much as to fay, with all my heart.

Jack. But Sir, my Grandmother wou'd never own me if I fhould change the curfen name fhe gave me with her own hands, an't pleafe your Worfhip.

Sir Sig. He *Beftia*! I'le have no more of your Worfhip, firrah, that old Englifh Sir Reverence, let me have you call me *Signior Illuftriffimo*, or *Patrona Mea*——or——

Tick. I, that I like well enough now :——but hold, fure this is one of your Mafters.

Enter Petro *dreft like a French Fencing Mafter.*

Pet. Signior *Barberacho* has fent me to teach you de Art of Fencing.

Sir Sig. Illuftriffimo Signior Monfieur, I am the Perfon who am to learn.

Tick. Stay Sir ftay,——let me ask him fome few queftions firft, for Sir *I* have play'd at Back-Sword and cou'd have handled ye a weapon as well as any man of my time in the Univerfity.

Sir Sig. Say you fo Mr. *Tickletext*, and I'faith you fhall have about with him.   [*Tick. Gravely goes to* Petro.

Tick. Hum——hum——Mr. *Monfieur*——pray what are the Guards that you like beft ?

Pet. Monfieur, eder de Quart or de Terfe, dey be both French and *Itallian* ; den for your Parades, degagements, your advancements, your Eloynements, and Retierments: dey be de fame ;

Tick. Cart and Horfe, what new found inventions and words have we here,——Sir *I* wou'd know, whether you like St. *Georges* Guard or not.

Pet. Alon——*Monfieur, Mette vous en Guard* ! take de Flurette.

Sir Sig. Nay faith and troth Governor thou fhat have a Rubbers with him.   [*Tick. Smiling refufes.*

Tick. Nay *certo* Sir Signal,——and yet you fhall prevail ;——well Sir, come your ways?   [*Takes the fluret.*

C   *Pet.*

Pet. Set your right foot forward, turn up your hand fo——dat be
de *Quart*——Now turn it dus——and dat be *de Terfe*.

Tick. Hocus, Pocus, Hickfius, Doxius——here be de Cart and here
be de Horfe—why what's all this for, hah Sir—and where's your guard
all this while?

Sir *Sig*. Ay Sir where's your Guard Sir, as my Governor fays, Sir,
hah?

Tick. Come, come, Sir, I muft inftruct you I fee—Come your ways
Sir.——

Pet. *A Tande a Tande um pew*,—truft de right hand and de right
leg forward together.——

Tick. I marry Sir, that's a good one indeed! what fhall become of
my head then Sir, what Guard have I left for that good Mr. *Monfieur*,
hah?

Pet. Ah Morblew, is not dis for every ting?

Tick. No marry is it not Sir, St. *Georges* Guard is the beft for your
head whilft you live,——as thus Sir.——

Pet. Dat Sir, ha ha——dat be Guard for de Back-Sword.

Tick. Back-fword Sir, yes, Back-fword, what fhould it be elfe.

Pet. And dis be de Single-Rapier.

Tick. Single-Rapier with a vengeance, there's a weapon for a
Gentleman indeed; is all this ftir about Single-Rapier?

Pet. Single-Rapier! What will you have for de Gentleman, de
Cudgell for de Gentleman?

Tick. No Sir, but I wou'd have it for de Rafcally French-man who
comes to abufe perfons of Quality with Paltry Single-Rapier.——Single
Rapier! Come Sir, come,——put your felf in your Cart and your
Horfe as you call it, and I'le fhew you the difference.

Vndreffes himfelf till he appears in a Ridiculous Pofture.

Pet. Ah *Monfieur* me fall run you two three times through de body,
and den you break a me head, what care I for dat :——Pox on his ignorance!   [*Afide*.

Tick. Oh ho Sir, do your worft Sir, do your worft Sir.

They put themfelves into feveral Guards, and Tick. *beats* Pet. *about
the Stage*——Enter Gall. Fill. *and* Jul.

Pet. Ah *Monfieur*, *Monfieur*, will you kill a me?

Tick. Ah *Monfieur* where be your Carts now and your Horfe, Mr.
Monfieur, hah!——and your Single-Rapier Mr. *Monfieur* hah!——

Gall. Why how now Mr. *Tickletext*, what mortal wars are thefe?
Ajax and *Uliffes* contending for *Achillis* his Armour?

Pet. If I be not reveng'd on him, hang me :   [*Afide*.

Sir *Sig*. Ay, why who the Devil wou'd have taken my Governor
for fo tall a man of hands, but *Corpo de me* Mr. *Galliard*, I have not
feen his Fellow.

                                                                Tick.

Tick. Ah Sir, time was, I wou'd have play'd ye a Match at Cudgells with e're a Sophister in the Colledge, but verily I have forgotten it, but here's an impudent French-man that wou'd have paft Single-Rapier upon us.

Gall. How, nay a my word then he deferv'd to be chaftis'd for't.——but now all's at peace again; Pray know my kinfman, Sir *Harry Fillamour.*

Sir *Sig.* *Yo baco les manos,* Signior *Illuftriffimo Cavaliero,*——and yours Signiors who are *Multo bien Venito ;*

Tick. Oh Lord Sir, you take me Sir——in fuch a pofture Sir——as I proteft I have not been feen in this many years.

[*Dreffing himfelf whilft he talks.*

Fill. Exercife is good for health Sir.

Gall. Sir *Signal,* you are grown a perfect Itallian ? Well Mr. *Tickletext* you will carry him home a moft accomplifh't Gentleman I fee !

Tick. Hum, verily Sir though I fay it, for a man that never travell'd before, I think I have done reafonably well ;——I'le tell you Sir——it was by my directions and advice, that he brought over with him,——two Englifh knives, a thoufand of Englifh pins, four pair of Jerfey ftockings, and as many pair of Buck-skin Gloves.

Sir *Sig.* Ay Sir, for good Gloves you know are very fcarce comodities in this Country.

Jul. Here Sir at *Rome,* as you fay, above all other places.

Tick. *Certo* meer hedging-Gloves Sir, and the clouterleft feams.——

Fill. Very right Sir,——and now he talks of *Rome,*——Pray Sir give me your opinion of the place?——are there not Noble buildings here ? rare ftatues, and admirable Fountains ?

Tick. Your buildings are pretty buildings, but not comparable to our Univerfity-buildings ; your Fountains I confefs are pretty Springs, – and your ftatues reafonably well carv'd——but Sir, they are fo ancient they are of no vallue ! then your Churches are the worft that ever I faw——that ever I faw.

Gall. How Sir, the Churches, why I thought *Rome* had been famous throughout all *Europe* for fine Churches.

Fill. What think you of St. *Peters* Church Sir, Is it not a glorious ftructure ?

Tick. St. *Peters* Church Sir, you may as well call it St. *Peters* Hall Sir ; it has neither Pew, Pullpit, Desk, Steeple, nor Ring of Bells, and call you this a Church Sir? no Sir, I'le fay that for little *England,* and a fig for't, for Churches, eafy Pulpits [Sir *Sig. fpeaks,* and fleeping Pews,] they are as well order'd as any Churches in Chriftiandom : and finer Rings of Bells Sir, I'am fure were never heard.

Jul. Oh Sir there's much in what you fay.

Fill.

Fill. But then Sir, your Rich Altars, and excellent Pictures of the greateſt Maſters of the World, your delicate Muſick, and Voices, make ſome amends for the other wants.

Tick. How Sir ! tell me of your Rich Altars, your guegaws and trinkets, and Popiſh Foperies! with a deal of ſing-ſong—when I ſay give me Sir five hundred cloſe changes rung by a ſet of good Ringers, and I'le not exchange 'em for all the Anthens in *Europe* : and for the Pictures Sir, they are ſuperſtition, Idolatrous, and flat Popery.

Fill. I'le convince you of that errour that perſwades you harmleſs Pictures are Idolatrous.

Tick. How Sir, how Sir, convince me, talk to me of being convinc't and that in favour of Popery ; No Sir, by your favour I ſhall not be convinc't, convinc't quoth a——No Sir far you well an you be for convincing, come away Sir *Signall*, far you well Sir, far you well——convin'ct. *[goes out.*

Sir *Sig.* Ha, ha, ha, ſo now is my Governor gone in a Fuſtian-fume, well, he is ever thus when one talks of whoring and Religion, but come Sir walk in, and I'le undertake my Tutor ſhall beg your pardon and renounce his Engliſh ill-bred opinion ; Nay, his Engliſh Churches too.——all but his own Vicaridge.

Fill. I have better diverſion Sir I thank you——come *Julio,* are you for a walk in the Garden of *Medices Villa,* 'tis hard by ?——

Jul. I'le wait on you—— *[Ex.* Fill. *and* Julio.

Sir *Sig.* How in the Garden of *Medices Villa*——but harkey *Galliard,* will the Ladies be there, the Curtizans ! the *bona roba's,* the *inamorata's,* and the *Bell ingrato's,* hah ?

Gall. Oh doubtleſs Sir; *[Ex.* Gall.

Sir *Sig.* I'le ene bring my Governor thither to beg his Pardon, on purpoſe to get an Opportunity to ſee the fine Women ; it may be I may get a ſight of my new Miſtreſs, *Dona Silvianetta* whom *Petro* is to bring me acquainted with. *[Exeunt.*

ACT II. SCENE I.

Enter Murismi *and* Octavio.

Oct. **B**Y Heaven I will not Eat, nor sleep, nor pray for any thing but swift and sure Revenge, till I have found *Marcella*, that false deceiving Beauty or her Lover, my hated Rival *Fillamour*! who wanton in the Arms of the fair Fugitive laughs at my shamefull easiness, and crys, these joys were never meant for tame *Octavio*!

Enter Crapine.

Mur. How now *Crapine*! What no news, no news of my Neeces yet, *Marcella* nor *Cornelia*?

Crap. None Sir.

Oct. That's wondrous strange, *Rome's* a place of that general Intelligence, methinks thou might'st have news of such Trivial things as women, amongst the Cardinals Pages; I'le undertake to learn the Region *de stato*, and present juncture of all affairs in *Italy* of a common Curtizan.

Mur. Sirrah-sirrah, let be it your care to examine all the Nunnerys, for my own part not a petticoat shall escape me.——

Oct. My task shall be for *Fillamore*.   [*Aside.*

Mur. I'le only make a visit to your sister *Dona Laura Lucretia*, and deliver her a Letter from my Nephew *Julio*, and return to you presently.——   [*Going out, is stay'd by* Octavio.

Oct. Stay Sir, defer your visit to my sister *Laura*, she is not yet to know of my being in Town, 'tis therefore I have taken a lodging in an obscure street, and am resolv'd never to be my self again till I've redeem'd my Honour. Come Sir, lets walk.——

Enter to them as they are going out, Marcella *and* Cornelia, *drest like Curtizans,* Philipa *and attendance.*

Mur. Stay stay, what women are these?

Oct. Whores Sir, and so 'tis ten to one are all the kind, only these differ from the rest in this, they generously own their trade of sin, which others deal by stealth in: they are Curtizans.   [*Exeunt.*

Mar. The Evenings soft and calm, as happy Lovers thoughts: And here are Groves where the kind meeting Trees Will hide us from the Amourous gazing croud.

Cor. What shou'd we do there, sigh till our wandering Breath, Has rais'd a gentle gale amongst the boughs; To whose dull melancholly Musick, we

Laid on a Bed of Mofs, and new fall'n leaves,
Will reade the difmall tale of Eccho's Love !
——No, I can make better ufe of Famous *Ovid* !

[*Snatches a little Book from her.*

And prethee what a pox have we to do with Trees,
Flowers, Fountains, or naked ftatues ?

Mar. But prethee mad *Cornelia* lets be grave and wife, at leaft e-
nough to think a little.

Cor. On what ? your Englifh Cavalier, *Fillamour*, of whom you tell
fo many dull ftories of his making Love ! Oh how I hate a civil whining Coxcomb !

Mar. And fo do I, I'le therefore think of him no more.

Cor. Good Lord ! what a damnable wicked thing is a Virgin grown
up to woman.

Mar. Why art thou fuch a fool, to think I love this *Fillamour ?*

Cor. It may be not at *Rome*, but at *Vitterbo*, where men are fcarce
you did ; and did you follow him to *Rome*, to tell him you cou'd Love
no more ?

Mar. A too forward Maid *Cornelia*, hurts her own fame, and that
of all her fex.

Cor. Her Sex, a pretty confideration by my youth, an Oath I fhall
not violate this dozen year, my fex fhou'd excufe me, if to preferve
their fame, they expected I fhou'd ruin my own quiet : in chufing an
ill favourd Husband, fuch as *Octavio* before a young handfome Lover,
fuch as you fay *Fillamour* is.

Mar. I wou'd fain perfwade my felf to be of thy minde,——but the
World *Cornelia.*——

Cor. Hang the malicious World——

Mar. And there's fuch charms, in wealth and Honour too !

Cor. None half fo powerfull as Love, in my opinion, 'life Si fer thou
art beautifull, and haft a Fortune too, which before I wou'd lay out
upon fo fhamefull a purchafe as fuch a Bedfellow for life as *Octavio* ; *I*
wou'd turn errant keeping Curtizan, and buy my better fortune.

Mar. That word too ftartles me.

Cor. What Curtizan, why 'tis a Noble title and has more *Votaries*
then Religion, there's no Merchandize like ours, that of Love my fifter !
——and can you be frighted with the vizor, which you your felf put on !

Mar. 'Twas the only difguife that cou'd fecure us from the fearch
of my Uncle and *Octavio,* our Brother *Julio* is by this too arriv'd, and
I know they'l all be dilligent,——and fome honour I was content to facri-
cife to my eternal repofe.

Cor. Spoke like my fifter, a little impertinent Honour, we may
chance to lofe 'tis true, but our right down honefty, I perceive you are
refolv'd we fhall maintain through all the dangers of Love and Gal-
lantry ;

lantry ;——though to fay truth I finde enough to do, to defend my heart againſt ſome of thoſe Members that Nightly ſerinade us : and daily ſhow themſelves before our window, Gay as young Bridegrooms and as full of expectation.

Mar. But is't not wondrous, that amongſt all theſe crowds we ſhould not once ſee *Fillamour,* I thought the charms of a fair young Curtizan, might have oblig'd him to ſome curioſity at leaſt.

Cor. Ay ! and an Engliſh Cavalier too, a Nation ſo fond of all new Faces.

Mar. Heaven, if I ſhould never ſee him, and I frequent all publique places to meet him ; or if he be gone from *Rome,* if he have forgot me, or ſome other Beauty have imploy'd his thoughts !——

Cor. Whe if all theſe if's and or's come to paſs, we have no more to do then to advance in this ſame glorious Profeſſion, of which now we only ſeem to be : ——in which to give it its due, there are a thouſand ſatisfactions to be found, more then in a dull virtuous life ! Oh the world of dark Lanthorn men we ſhou'd have ; the Serinades, the Songs, the ſighs, the Vows, the Preſents, the quarels, and all for a look or a ſmile, which you have been hitherto ſo covetous of, that *Petro* ſwears our Lovers begins to ſuſpect us for ſome honeſt gilts ; which by ſome is accounted much the lewder ſcandal of the two, ——therefore I think faith we muſt ene be kinde a little, to redeem our reputations.

Mar. However we may rally, certainly there's nothing ſo hard· to woman, as to expoſe her ſelf to villainous Man.

Cor. Faith Siſter, if 'twere but as eaſy to ſatisfy the nice ſcruples of Religion, and Honour, I ſhould finde no great difficulty in the reſt,—— beſides another argument I have, our money's all gone, and without a Miracle can hold out no longer honeſtly.——

Mar. Then we muſt ſell our Jewels !

Cor. When they are gone, what Jewell will you part with next.

Mar. Then we muſt. ——

Cor. What, go home to *Vitterbo,* ask the Old Gentleman pardon, and be receiv'd to Grace again, you to the embraces of the amiable *Octavio* ; and I to St. *Teretia's,* to whiſtle through a Grate like a Bird in a Cage,——for I ſhall have little heart to ſing :——but come let's leave this ſad talk, here's men——let's walk and gain new Conqueſt, I love it dearly.—— [*Walk down the Garden.*

Enter Gall. Fill. *and* Jul. *See the Women.*

Gall. Women ! and by their garbo for our purpoſe too——they're Curtizans, lets follow 'em.

Fill. What ſhall we get by gazing but diſquiet, if they are fair and honeſt, we look and perhaps may ſigh in vain ; if beautiful and looſe, they are not worth regarding.

Gall.

Gall. Dear Notional Knight, leave your ſatirical Foperies, and be at leaſt good humour'd, and let's follow 'em.

Jul. I'le leave you in the purſuit, and take this opportunity, to write my Uncle word of my arrival : and wait on you here anon.

Fill. Prethee do ſo : hah, whoſe that with ſuch an equipage ?

[*Exit.* Jul. Fill. *and* Gall. *going after.* Marcella *and* Cor. *meet juſt entring,* Laura *with her Equipage, dreſt like a man.*

Gall. Pox, let the Tradeſmen ask, who cringe for ſuch gay Cuſtomers, and follow us the women !

[*Exit* Fill. *and* Gall. *down the ſcene.* Lau. *looking after 'em.*

Laur. 'Tis he, my Cavalier ! my Conqueror : *Antonio,* let the Coaches wait !——and ſtand at diſtance all ! Now *Silvio,* on thy life forget my Sex and quality, forget my uſeleſs Name of *Laura Lucretia,* and call me Count of——

Silv. What Madam ?

Lau. Madam ! ah fooliſh Boy ? thy feminine courage will betray us all;——but——call me——Count——*San's Ceure;*——and tell me *Silvio,* How is it I appear !
How doſt thou like my ſhape——my face and dreſs ?
My Mien and Equipage, may I not paſs for man ?
Looks it *en Prince,* and Maſculine,

Silv. Now as I live you look all over what you wiſh ; and ſuch, as will beget a reverance and Envy in the men, and Paſſion in the women, but what's the cauſe of all this transformation ?

Lau. Love ! Love ! Dull boy, cou'dſt thou not gueſs 'twas Love ? that dear Engleſe I muſt enjoy my *Silvio.*

Silv. What he that adores the fair young Curtizan.

Lau. That very he, my window joyns to hers, and 'twas with charms Which he'ad prepar'd for her, he took this heart,
Which met the wellcome Arrows in their flight.
And ſav'd her from their dangers,
Oft I've returnd the vows he'as made to her
And ſent him pleas'd away ;
When through the Errours of the Night, and diſtance
He has miſtook me for that happy wanton,
And gave me Language of ſo ſoft a Power,
As ne're was breath'd in vain to liſtening Maids.

Silv. But with permiſſion, Madam, how does this change of Petticote for Britches, and ſhifting houſes too, advance that Love ?

Lau. This habit, beſides many opportunities 'twill give me, of geting into his acquaintance, ſecures me to from being known by any of my Relations in *Rome* ; then I have chang'd my houſe for one ſo neer to that of *Silvianettas,* and ſo like it too, that even you and I have oft miſtook the entrance ; by which means Love, Fortune, or
Chance ;

chance, may with my induſtry contrive ſome kinde miſtake that may make me happyer then the reſt of woman kinde.

Silv. But what ſhall be reſerv'd then for Count *Julio*, whoſe laſt letters promiſe his arrival within a day or two, and whom you're then to Marry?

Lau. Reſerv'd for him! a wife! a wife my *Silvio*,
That unconcern'd Domeſtique Neceſſary,
Who rarely brings a heart, or takes it ſoon away:

Silv. But then your Brother Count *Octavio*, do you not fear his jealouſie?

Lau. Octavio! Oh Nature has ſet his Soul and mine at odds,
And I can know no fear, but where I Love!

Silv. And then that thing that Ladys call their Honour——

Lau. Honour, That hated Idoll, even by thoſe
That ſet it up to worſhip: No,
I have a Soul my Boy, and that's all Love! ~
And I'le the Tallent which Heaven lent improve?

  [*Going out, meets* Marcella *and* Cornelia *followed by* Gall. *and* Fill.

Sil. Here be the Curtizans, my Lord?

Lucr. Hah, *Silvianetta* and *Euphemia*! purſu'd too by my Cavalier,
I'le round the Garden, and mix my ſelf amongſt 'em,

     [*Exeunt with her train.*

Mar. Prethee Siſter let's retire into the grove, to avoid the purſuit of theſe Cavaliers?

Cor. Not I, by theſe killing Eyes! I'le ſtand my ground were there a thouſand, all Arm'd with Conquering Beauty?

Mar. Hah——Now on my Conſcience yonders *Fillamour*!

Cor. Ha! *Fillamour*!

Mar. My courage fails me at the ſight of him——I muſt retire.

Cor. And I'le too my Art of Love!

  [Mar. *retires and leans againſt a Tree,* Cor. *walks about reading.*

Gall. 'Tis ſhe, 'tis *Silvianetta*! Prethee advance that thou maiſt behold her and renounce all honeſt women: ſince in that one young ſinner there are charms, that wou'd excuſe even to thee all frailty;

Fill. The forms of Angells cou'd not reconcile me
To women of her trade.

Gall. This is too happy an opportunity, to be loſt in convincing thy ſingularity,—— [Gall. *goes bowing by the ſide of* Cornelia, Fill.
      walks about in the Scene.

——If creatures ſo fair and charming, as your ſelf had any need of prayer, I ſhou'd believe by your profound attention you were at your Evenings Devotion.

Cor. That you may finde your miſtake, in the opinion of my charms, Pray believe I am ſo, and ought not to be interrupted.

Gall. I hope a Man may have leave to make his Devotions by you,
       D   at

at leaſt, without danger or offence?

Cor. I know not that, I have reaſon to fear your devotion may be ominous, like a Blazing Star, it comes but ſeldom,——but ever threatens miſchief,——Pray Heaven I ſnare not in the calamity:

Gall. Whe I confeſs Madam, my fit of zeal does not take me often, but when it does, 'tis very harmleſſe and wondrous hearty.——

Cor. You may begin then, I ſhall not be ſo wicked as to diſturb your Oriſons.

Gall. Wou'd I cou'd be well aſſur'd of that, for mine's devotion of great neceſſity, and the bleſſing I pray infinitely for, conſerves me; therefore in Chriſtian Charity keep down your eyes, and do not ruine a young mans good intentions, unleſſe they wou'd agree to ſend kinde looks, and ſave me the expence of prayer.

Cor. Which wou'd be better laid out you think upon ſome other bleſſing.

Gall. Whe faith 'tis good, to have a little bank upon occaſion, though I hope I ſhall have no great need hereafter,——if the charming *Silvianetta* be but kinde, 'tis all I ask of Heaven.

Cor. You're very well acquainted with my Name I find!

Gall. Your Name! 'tis all I have to live on!
Like cheerfull Birds, 'tis the firſt tune I ſing,
To wellcome in the day:
The Groves repeat it, and the Fountains Purle it,
And every pretty ſound that fills my ear,
Turns all to *Silvianetta*!   [*Fill. looks a while on* Marcella.

Fill. Galliard, look there——look on that lovely woman; 'tis *Marcella*! the Beautifull *Marcella*!   [*Offers to run to her,* Gall. *holds him.*

Gall. Hold! *Marcella*! where?

Fill. That Lady there! did'ſt ever ſee her equall?

Gall.——Whe faith as you ſay *Harry*, that Lady is beautifull——and make us thankfull——kinde, whe 'tis *Euphenia* Sir, the very Curtizan, I wou'd have ſhow'd you.——

Fill. Forbear, I am not fit for mirth.

Gall. Nor I in humour to make you merry;
I tell ye——yonder woman——is a Curtizan.

Fill. Do not prophane nor rob Heaven of a Saint!

Gall. Nor you rob mankinde of ſuch a bleſſing, by giving it to Heaven before its time.——I tell thee 'tis a whore! a fine deſirable expenſive whore.

Fill. By Heaven it cannot be! I'le ſpeak to her, and call her my *Marcella*, and undeceive thy leud opinion.   [*Offers to go, he holds him.*

Gall. Do, ſalute her in good Company for an honeſt woman——do ——and ſpoil her markets: ——'twill be a pretty civil ſpightful Complement, and no doubt well taken;——come I'le convince ye Sir,
            [*Goes and pulls* Philipa.
               ——Hearkey

——Harkey thou kinde help-meet for man——thou gentle childe of Night——What is the price of a Night or two of pleasure, with yonder Lady——*Euphemia*, I mean, that Roman Curtizan.——

Fill. Oh Heavens! a Curtizan!

Phil. Sure you're a great stranger in *Rome*, that cannot tell her price.

Gall. I am so——Name it prethee, here's a young English purchaser——Come forward man, and cheapen for your self,—— [*Pulls him.*

Phil. Oh spare your pains, she wants no customers.——[*slings away.*

Fill. No No, it cannot, must not be, *Marcella*!
She has too much Divinity about her,
Not to defend her from all imputation,
Scandal wou'd die to hear her name pronounc't.

Phil. Believe me, Madam, he knows you not, I overheard all he said to that Cavalier, and finde he's much in Love!

Mar. Not know me, and in love! punish him Heaven for falshood! but I'le contribute to deceive him on, and ruin him with perjury.

Fill. I am not yet convinc't, I'le try her farther! [*Goes to her bowing.*
——but, Madam, is that Heavenly beauty purchasable? I'le pay a heart rich with such wounds, and flames.——

Gall. Not forgetting the Money too good lad, or your wounds and flames will be of little use! [*Gall. goes to* Cornelia.

Mar. He tells you truth, Sir, we are not like the Ladies of your Country, who tire out their men with loving upon the square, heart for heart, till it becomes as dull as Matrimony, to women of our profession there's no Rethorick like ready Money, nor Billet-Doux like Bill of Exchange.

Fill. Oh! that Heaven shou'd make two persons so resembling, And yet such different souls———— [*Looks on her.*
——'sdeath how she darts me through with every look,
But if she speak she heals the wound again:

Enters Octavio, *with followers.*

Octa. Hah, my Rival *Fillamour* here! fall on——draw Sir,——and say I gave you one advantage more and fought thee fairly.

[*Draws on* Fill. Fill. *fights him out* ; *the Ladies run off* : Gall. *Falls on the followers, with whom whilst he is ingaged, Enters* Julio, *draws and assists him* : *and* Laura *at the same time on the other side* ; *Enter* Petro *drest like a Civility-Master* ; *Sir* Signal *and* Tickletext, *Sir* Signal *climbs a Tree* ; Tick.*runs his head in a bush, and lies on his hands and knees,* Pet. *assists* Gall. *and fights out the Bravo's* : Pet. *re-Enters.*

Lau. Hah my Cavalier ingag'd amongst the slaves.

Pet. My Ladys Lovers! and set upon by *Octavio*! we must be dilligent in our affairs! Sir *Signal* where are ye! *Signior Tickletext*! I hope they have not miscarried in the fray?

Sir Sig. Oh *vot Servitor vos Signoria,* mifcarried, no the fool has wit enough to keep out of harms way.　　　　[*Comes down from the Tree:*

Pet. Oh very difcreetly done Signior. ——

　　　　　　　[*Sees* Tick. *in a bufh, pulls him out by the heels.*

Sir Sig. Whe how now Governor what afraid of fwords.

Tick. No Sir, I am not afraid of Swords, but I am afraid of danger.

　　　　[*Enter.* Gall. *embracing* Laura *! after'em,* Jul. *and* Fill.
　　　　　　Fill. *looks about..*

Gall. This bravery Sir was wondrous !

Lau. 'Twas only juftice Sir you being oppreft with odds.

Fill. She's gone ! fhe's gone in Triumph with my Soul.

Jul. What was the matter Sir, how came this mifchief ?

Fill. Oh eafily Sir ; I did but look, and infinitly lov'd !

Jul. And therefore were you drawn upon, or was it fome old Pique?

Fill. I know not Sir, Oh tell not me of quarrels.
The woman friend, the woman has undone me !

Gall. Oh a bleffed hearing ! I'me glad of the reformation Sir, you were fo fquemifh forfooth, that a whore wou'd not down with ye ! no, 'twou'd fpoil your Reputation.——

Fill. A whore ! wou'd I cou'd be convinc't fhe were fo, 'twou'd call my Virtue home and make me man again !

Gall. Thou ly'ft ——thou'rt as weak a Brother as the beft on's, and believe me *Harry,* thefe fort of Damfells are like witches, if they once get hold of a man, he's their own till the charm be ended ; you guefs what that is Sir ?

Fill. Oh *Frank,* hadft thou then felt how tenderly fhe preft my hand in hers ; as if fhe wou'd have kept there for ever, it wou'd have made thee mad, ftark mad in Love !——and nothing but *Marcella* cou'd have charm'd me ;　　　　　　　　　　　　[*Afide.*

Gall. Ay Gad, I'le warrant thee,——well thou fhalt this night enjoy her.

Fill. How !

Gall. How, Whe faith *Harry,* ene the old way, I know no other. Whe thou fhalt ly with her man ! come let's to her.

Fill. Away, let's follow her inftantly.　[*Going out, ftopt by Sir* Signal.

　　　　　　Enter Sir Sig. Tick. Petro.

Sir Sig. Signior, I have brought Mr. *Tickletext,* to beg your pardon——Sir.

Fill. I've other bufinefs Sir.　　　　　　　　　[*Goes out.*

Gall. Come let's follow him, and you my generous Cavalier, muft give me leave to beg the Honour of your friendfhip.

Lau. My inclinations Sir, have given you more——pray let me wait on you to your Lodgings, left a farther infolence fhou'd be offer'd you.

　　　　　　　　　　　　　　　　　　　　Gall.

Gall. Sir you oblige too faſt ; [*They go out.*

Sir *Sig.* Ah *che Deavilo Ayles* theſe hot-brain'd fellows, ſure they're Drunk.

Pet, Oh ſee Signior, Drunk, for a man of Quality—'tis intollerable.

Sir *Sig.* Ay : Whe how ſo Signior *Morizoroſo.*

Pet. Imbriaco, had made it a fine ſpeech indeed.

Sir *Sig.* Whe faith, and ſo it had, as thus,——*ach Deavilo Ailes* theſe hot-brain'd fellows, ſure they are *imbriaco,*——now wou'd not I be Drunk for a thouſand Crowns : *imbriacho* ſounds *Cinqant par cent* better,——Come Noble Signior, let's *Andiamo a Caſa,* which is as much as to ſay, let's amble home.——

Tick. Introth, wondrous expert——*Certo* Signior he's an apt Schollar,

Sir *Sig.* Ah Sir, you ſhall ſee, when I come to my civillities.——

Pet. Where the firſt leſſon you ſhall learn, is, how to give, and how to receive, with a Bon-Grace !

Tick. That receiving leſſon I will learn my ſelf ;

Pet. This unfrequented part of the Garden, Signior will fit our pur-poſe as well as your Lodgings,——Firſt then——Signiors your addreſs,
                                         [*Puts himſelf in the middle.*
                [Petro *bows on both ſides, they do the like.*
——Very well ! that's at the approach of any perſon of Quality ; after which you muſt take out your Snuff-Box.

Sir *Sig.* Snuff-Box : whe we take no ſnuff Signior.

Pet. Then Sir by all means you muſt learn : for beſides the mode and gravity of it, it inviveates the *Pericranium* ! that is ſapientiat's the brain,——that is, inſpires wit, thought, invention, underiſtanding, and the like——you conceive me Signiors——   [*Bowing.*

Sir *Sig.* Moſt profoundly Signior.——   [*Bowing.*

Pet.——Then Signiors, it keeps you in confidance, and countinance ! and whilſt you gravely ſeem to take a ſnuſh, you gain time to anſwer to the purpoſe, (and in a politique poſture——as thus.)——to any in-tricate queſtion.

Tick. Hum——*certo* I like that well ; and 'twere admirable if a man were allow'd to take it when he's out in's Sermon.

Pet. Doubtleſs Signior you might, it helps the memory better then Roſemary, therefore I have brought each of you a Snuff-Box.

Sir *Sig.* By no means : Excuſe me Signior.   [*Refuſes to take 'em.*

Pet. Ah Bagatells Signior, Bagatells, and now Signiors, I'le teach you how to take it, with a handſome Grace, Signior your hand ;—— and yours Signior.   [*Lays ſnuff on their hands.*
——So now draw your hand to, and frow under your Noſes, and ſnuff it hard up :——Excellent well,
           [*They dawb all their Noſes, and make grimaces and ſneeze.*

Sir *Sig.* Methinks Signior, this ſnuff ſtinks moſt damnably : Pray what ſcent do you call this ?

                                         Pet.

Pet. Cackamarda Orangate, a rare perfume I'le aſſure ye, Sir.

Sir *Sig.* Cackamarda Orangate, and 'twere not for the Name of *Cackamarda,* and ſo forth, a man had as good have a Sir Reverence at his Noſe.   [*Sneezes, often he crys bonprovache.*

Pet. Bonprovache——Signior, you do not underſtand it yet, bonprovache.

Sir *Sig.* Whe Sir 'tis impoſſible to endure this ſame *Cackamarda,* Whe Aſſaffetteda is Odoriferous to it.   [*Sneezing.*

Pet. 'Tis your right *Dulce Piquante,* believe me :——but come Signiors wipe your Noſes and proceed to your giving leſſon.

Sir *Sig.* As how Signior.

Pet. Whe——preſent we with ſomething——that——Diamond on your finger ! to ſhew the manner of giving handſomely :
[*Sir* Sig. *gives it him.*
——Oh fy, Signior——between your Finger and Thumb——thus—— with your other Fingers at a diſtance——with a ſpeech, and a bow.——

Sir *Sig. Iluſtriſſimo* Signior, the Manifold Obligations.——

Pet. Now a fine turn of your hand——thus——Oh that ſets off the preſent, and makes it ſparkle in the eyes of the receiver.——
[*Sir* Sig. *turns his hand.*

Sir *Sig.*——Which you have heap't upon me,——

Pet. There flouriſh again.   [*He flouriſhes.*

Sir *Sig.* Obliges me to beg, your acceptance of this ſmall preſent, which will receive a double Luſtre from your fair hand.   [*Gives it him.*

Pet. Now kiſs your fingers ends, and retire back with a bow :

Tick.——Moſt admirably perform'd.

Sir *Sig.* Nay Sir I have docity in me, tho' I ſay't : come Governor let's ſee how you can out-do me in the Art of preſenting.

Tick. Well Sir, come, your ſnuff-Box will ſerve inſtead of my Ring, will it not ?

Pet. By no means Sir, there is ſuch a certain Relation between a Finger and a Ring, that no preſent becomes either the giving or the receiving hand half ſo well.

Sir *Sig.* Whe 'twill be reſtor'd again, 'tis but to practice by.

Pet. Ay Signior, the next thing you are to learn is to receive.

Tick. Moſt worthy Signior, I have ſo Exhauſted the *Cornucopia* of your favours, [*Flouriſhes*]——and taſted ſo plenteouſly of the fullneſſe of your Bounteous Liberallity, that to retalliate with this ſmall Jem——is but to offer a ſpark, where I have received a beam of ſuperabundant ſun-ſhine.——   [*Gives it.*

Sir *Sig.* Moſt Rhetorically perform'd, as I hope to breath, Tropes and fugers all over.

Tick. Oh Lord, Sir *Signal.*

Pet. Excellent——Now let's ſee if you can refuſe, as civilly as you gave, which is by an Obſtinate denial ; ſtand both together,——

——Iluſtrious

——Iluftrious Signiors, upon my honour my little merrit has not inti-
tled me to the Glory of fo fplendid an offering ; Trophes worthy to
be laid only at your Magnanimous feet.

Sir *Sig*. Ah Signior, No No,

Pet. Signior *Tickletext*.   [*He offers, they refufe going backward.*

Tick. Nay *certo* Signior ! ——

Pet. With what confidence can I receive fo rich a prefent : Signior
Tickletext, ah——Signior.——

Sir *Sig*. I vow Signior——I'me afhamed you fhou'd offer it.

Tick. In verity, and fo am I.   [*ftill going back, he follows.*

Pet. *Pardio* ! *Baccus*, moft incomparable.——

Tick. But when Signior are we to learn to receive again.——

Pet. Oh Sir that's always a leffon of it felf :——but now Signiors,
I'le teach you how to Act a ftory.

Sir *Sig*. How ! how Signior to Act a ftory ?

Pet. Ay Sir, No matter for words or fenfe, fo the body perform its
part well.

Sir *Sig*. How, tell a ftory without words, whe this were an excellent devife for Mr. *Tickletext*, when he's to hold forth to the Congregation, and has loft his Sermon-Notes——whe this is wonderfull.——

Pet. Oh Sir, I have taught it men born deaf, and blinde,——look ye
ftand clofe together, and obferve——clofer yet: [*Gets between 'em.*
——a certain Eclejaftio, Plump, and Rich——[*Makes a figne of being fat.*
Riding along the Rode,——meets a   [*Galloping about the Stage.*
Paver ftrapiao, ——un Pavero ftrapiao, Paure ftrapiao :——ftrapiao
——ftrapiao——ftrapiao : ——   [*Puts himfelf into the Pofture of a lean*
Elemofuna per un Faure   *Beggar ; his hands right down by his*
ftrapiao, par a Moure de   *fides,— and picks both their Pockets.*
Dievos——at laft he begs a Julio——Neinte! [*Makes the fat Bifhop*]
——then the Paure ftrapiao begs a Mezo Julio——[*lean*] Neinte [*fat*]
——une bacio—[*kan*]—Niente— [*fat*] — at laft he begs his Bleffing——and fee how willingly the Eclefiaftico gave his Benediction ;
                              [*Opening his Arms hits them both in the face.*
——Scufa fcufa mea Patrona's——   [*Begs their pardon.*

Sir *Sig*. Yes very willingly, which by the way he had never done
had it been worth a farthing.

Tick. Marry I won'd he had been a little fparing of that too, at this
time,—[*fneezes*] a fhame on't, it has ftur'd this fame *Cackamerda* a-
gain moft foully.

Pet. Your pardon Signior, —— but come Sir *Signall* —let's fee how
you will make this filent relation——Come ftand between us two—

Sir *Sig*. Nay let me alone for a memory—come.

Pet. I think I have reveng'd my Backfword-beating.   [*goes off.*

Sir *Sig*. Un paureo ftrapado——plump and rich——no, no, the Eccle-
fiaftico meets un paureo ftrapado——and begs a *Julio*.

                                                  Tick.

Tick. Oh no Sir, the ſtrapado begs the *Julio.*

Sir *Sig.* Ay, Ay, and the Eclefaſtico crys Niente— [*ſnaps his nail.* un meze Julio!—Niente—un Bacoi, Niente, your bleſſing then Signior Ecclefaſtico   [*ſpreads out his arms to give his bleſſing—and hits* Tick.

Tick. Adds me, you are all a little too liberal of this fame bene-diction.

Sir *Sig.* Hah—but where's Signior *Morigoroſo?* what is he gone? —but now I think on't 'tis a point of good manners to go without ta-king leave.

Tick. It may be ſo, but I wiſh I had my Ring again, I do not like the giving leſſon without the taking one, whe this is picking a mans pocket *certo.*

Sir *Sig.* Not ſo Governor, for then I had had a conſiderable loſſe : look ye here,—how—[*feeling in his Pocket*] how—[*in another*] how—gone? gone as I live ! my money Governor ! all the Gold *Barberacho* receiv'd of my Marchant to day—all gone.—

Tick. Hah—and mine—all my ſtock, the money which I thought to have made a preſent to the Gentlewoman, *Barberacho* was to bring me too—[*aſide*]—nndone undone—Villains, Cutpurſes—Cheats, oh run after him.

Sir *Sig.* A Pox of all ſilent ſtories : Rogue, Thief—undone.—

ACT III. SCENE I.

Enter Julio *and his Page.*

Jul. HOw ! the Lady whom I followed from St. *Peters* Church a Curtizan?

Pag. A Curtizan my Lord, fair as the Morning, and as young.

Jul. I know ſhe's fair and young, but is ſhe to be had boy ?

Pag. My Lord ſhe is —her Footman told me, ſhe was a Zittella.

Jul. How a Zittella !—a Virgin, 'tis impoſſible.

Pag. I cannot ſwear it Sir, but ſo he told me ? he ſaid ſhe had a world of Lovers : her Name is *Silvianetta* Sir, and her Lodgings—

Jul. I know't, are on the *Corſo*; a Curtizan ! and a Zittella too ? a pretty contradiction ! but I'le bate her the laſt, ſo I might enjoy her as the firſt, what ere the price be, I'me reſolv'd upon the adventure; and will this minute prepare my ſelf. [*Going off, enters* Mur. *and* Octa. —hah—does the light deceive me, or is that indeed my Uncle, in earneſt conference with a Cavalier:—'tis he—I'le ſtep aſide till he's paſt, leſt he hinders this Nights diverſion :   [*Goes aſide*

Mur. I ſay 'twas raſhly done, to fight him unexamin'd.

Oct. I need not ask, my reafon has inform'd me, and I'me convinc't where ere he has conceald her, that fhe is fled with *Fillamour*.

Jul. Who is't they fpeak of?

Mar. Well well, fure my Anceftors committed fome horrid crime, againft Nature, that fhe fent this Peft of woman kind into our Family, ——two Neeces for my fhare,——by Heaven a proportion fufficient to undo fix Generations.

Jul. Hah ! two Neeces, what of them? 　　　　　　　[*Afide.*

Mur. I am like to give a bleffed account of 'em to their Brother *Julio* my Nephew, at his return, there's a new plague now,——but my comfort is I fhall be mad and there's an end on't. 　　　[*Weeps.*

Jul. My curiofity muft be fatisfied,——have patience Noble Sir,——

Mur. Patience is a flatterer Sir,——and an Afs Sir, and I'le have none on't——hah what art thou?

Jul. Has five or fix years, made ye lofe the remembrance of your Nephew——*Julio !*

Mur. Julio ! wou'd I had met thee going to thy Grave. 　　[*Weeps*

Jul. Why fo Sir?

Mur. Your fifters Sir, your fifters are both gone.—— 　　[*Weeps.*

Jul. How gone Sir?

Mur. Run away Sir, flown Sir.

Jul. Heavens ! which way?

Mur. Nay, who can tell the ways of fickle women,——in fhort Sir, your fifter *Marcella* was to have been Married, to this Noble Gentleman,——Nay was contracted to him, fairly contracted in my own Chappel, but no fooner was his back turn'd,——but in a pernicious Moon-light Night fhe fhews me a fair pair of heels, with the young Baggage your other fifter *Cornelia*, who was juft come from the Monaftery where I bred her, to fee her fifter married.

Jul. A curfe upon the Sex, why muft mans honour Depend upon their Frailty?
——Come——give me but any light which way they went,
And I will trace 'em with that carefull Vengeance.——

Oct. Spoke like a man, that underftands his Honour,
And I can guefs how we may finde the Fugitives.

Jul. Oh Name it quickly Sir!

Oct. There was a young Cavalier——fome time at *Vitterbo*, 　　　⁕
Who I confefs had charms, Heaven has denied to me
That trifle Beauty, which was made to pleafe,
Vain foolifh Woman, which the brave and wife,
Want leafure to defign:

Jul. And what of him !

Oct. This fine gay thing came in your fifters way, and made that conqueft Nature meant fuch fools for : and Sir fhe's fled with him.

Jul. Oh fhow me the Man, the daring hardy Villain,

E

Bring

Jul. Oh *Fillamour*, I've heard such killing news since last I left thee.

Fill. What prethee?

Jul. I had a sister Friend——dear as my life,
And bred with all the Virtues of her Sex;
No Vestals at the Holy fire employ'd themselves
In innocenter businesse then this Virgin;
Till Love! the Fatall Feaver of her heart,
Betraid her harmlesse hours:
And just upon the point of being Married,
The thief stole in, and Rob'd us of this treasure:
She's left her Husband, Parents, and her Honour,
And's fled with the base ruiner of her Virtue.

Fill. And lives the Villain durst affront ye thus?

Jul. He does!

Gall. Where, in what distant World?

Jul. I know not.

Fill. What is he call'd?

Jul. I know not neither,——some God direct me to the Ravisher!
And if he scape my rage!
May Cowards point me out, for one of their tame herd.

Fill. In all your quarells I must joyn my sword.

Gall. And if you want,---here's another Sir,---that though it be not
often drawn in anger, nor cares to be, shall not be idle in good company.

Jul. I thank ye both, and if I have occasion, will borrow their af-
sistance, but I must leave you for a minute, I'le wait on you anon.——

[*They all three walk as down the street talking,*
Enter Laura, *with her Equipage.*

Lau. Beyond my wish, I'me got into his Friendship,
But oh how distant Friendship is from Love!
That's all bestowed on the fair Prostitute!
——Ah *Silvio*, when he took me in his Armes,
Pressing my willing Bosome to his breast,
Kissing my cheek, calling me Lovely youth,
And wondering how such Beauty, and such bravery,
Met in a Man so young! ah then my Boy!
Then in that happy minute,
How neer was I to telling all my soul,
My blushes and my sighs, were all prepar'd

My.

My Eyes caft down my trembling lips juft parting,——
But ftill as I was ready to begin,
He crys out *Silvianetta* !
And to prevent mine, tells me all his Love !
——But fee——he's here.——   [Fill. *and* Gall. *coming up the fcene.*

Gall. Come lay by all fullen unrefolves ! for now the hour of the Berjeare approaches, Night, that was made for Lovers !
——Hah ! my dear *Sans Cœur* ? my life ! my foul ! my joy !
Thou art of my opinion !

Lau. I'me fure I am what are it be ?

Gall. Whe my Friend here, and I have fent and paid our Fine for a fmall Tenement of pleafure, and I'me for taking prefent poffeffion;
——but hold——if you fhou'd be a Rivall after all !

Lau. Not in your *Silvianetta* ! My Love has a Nice appetite,
And muft be fed with high uncommon delicates,
I have a Miftrefs Sir, of quality !
Fair ! as imagination, paints young Angells !
Wanton and gay as was the firft *Corina* .
That charm'd our beft of Poets,
Young as the Spring, and cheerfull as the Birds
That wellcome in the day !
Witty as fancy makes the Revelling Gods,
And equally as bounteous when fhe bleffes !

Gall. Ah for a fine young whore, with all thefe charms ! but that fame quality allays the joy, there's fuch a dam'd ado with the Obligation, that half the pleafures loft in Ceremony,
——Here ! for a thoufand Crowns I raign alone,
Revell all day in Love without controle.
——But come to our bufinefs, I have given order for Mufick, Dark Lanthorns, and Piftolls.   [*This while* Fill. *ftands ftudying.*

Fill.——Death if it fhou'd not be *Marcella* now !   [*Paufing afide.*

Gall. Prethee no more confidering,——refolve and let's about it.

Fill. I wou'd not tempt my heart again ! for Love
What ere it may be in anothers breaft,
In mine, 'twill turn to a Religious fire !
And fo to burn for her ! a common Miftrefs,
Wou'd be an Infamy below her practice !

Gall. Oh if that be all, doubt not *Harry* but an hours converfation with *Euphemia,* will convert it to as lewd a flame, as a man wou'd wifh.

Lau. What a coyles here about a Curtizan ! what ado to perfwade a man to a bleffing all *Rome* is languifhing for in vain :——Come Sir, we muft deal with him, as Phyfitians do with peevifh children, force him to take what will cure him !

Fill. And like thofe dam'd Phyfitians, kill me for want of method, no, I know my own diftemper beft; and your applications will make me mad.   E 2   *Gall.*

Gall. Pox on't, that one cannot love a woman like a man, but one muſt love like an Aſs.

Lau. S'hart, I'le be bound to ly with all the women in *Rome*, with leſs ado then you are brought to one.

Gall. Hear ye that *Henry*, s'death art not aſham'd to be inſtructed by one ſo young!——but ſee——the ſtar there appears,—the ſtar that conduct thee to the ſhore of bliſs——

She comes let's feel thy   [Marcella *and* Cornelia *above.*
Heart ! ſhe comes !
So breaks the day on the glad Eaſtern Hills !
Or the bright God of Rays from *Thetis* Lap :——
A Rapture now dear lad, and then fall too, for thou art
Old dog at a long Grace.——

Fill. Now I'me meer man again, with all his frailties,—— [*Aſide.*
——Bright lovely creature !——

Gall. Damn it, how like my Ladys Eldeſt Son was that.

Fill. May I hope my ſacrifice ! may be accepted by you ?—by Heaven it muſt be ſhe ! ſtill ſhe appears more like.——   [*Aſide.*

Mar. I've only time to tell you Night approches, ·
And then I will expect you,   [*Enter* Crapine, *gazes on the Ladys.*

Crap. 'Tis ſhe, *Donna Marcella* on my life, with the young wild *Cornelia*!——hah——yonders the Engliſh Cavalier too, nay then by this hand I'le be paid for all my fruitleſs jants : for this good news——ſtay let me mark the Houſe.——

Mar. Now to my diſguiſe !   [*Ex.* Marcella.

Gall. And have you no kinde meſſage to ſend to my heart ; cannot this good Example, inſtruct you how to make me happy ?

Cor. Faith ſtranger I muſt conſider firſt, ſhe's skillfull in the Marchandize of hearts, and has dealt in Love with ſo good ſucceſs hitherto, ſhe may loſe on venture, and never miſs it in her ſtock, but this is my firſt, and ſhou'd it prove to be a bad bargain, I were undone for ever.

Gall. I dare ſecure the goods ſound,——

Cor. And I believe will not ly long upon my hands.

Gall. Faith, that's according as you'l diſpoſe on't Madam,—for let me tell you —gad a good handſome proper fellow, is as ſtaple a commodity as any's in the Nation,——but I wou'd be reſerv'd for your own uſe ! faith take a ſample to Night, and as you like it, the whole peece, and that's fair and honeſt dealing I think, or the Devils in't.

Cor. Ah ſtranger,——you have been ſo over-liberal of thoſe ſame ſamples of yours, that I doubt they have ſpoild the ſale of the reſt,—— cou'd you not afford think ye, to throw in a little Love and conſtancy ; to inch out that want of honeſty of yours.

Gall. Love ! oh in abundance !
By thoſe dear Eyes, by that ſoft ſmiling Mouth ;
By ever ſecret grace, thou haſt about thee,

I love thee with a vigorous, eager paffion,
——Be kinde dear *Silvianetta*—prethee do,
Say you believe and make me bleft to Night ?
. *Crap. Silvianetta*! fo, that's the Name fhe has rifl'd for *Cornelia, I*
perceive.

Cor. If I fhou'd be fo kind-hearted ! what good ufe wou'd you make
of fo obliging an opportunity ?

Gall. That which the happy Night was firft ordain'd for.

Cor. Well Signior 'tis coming on, and then I'le try what courage
the darknefs will infpire me with:——till then——farwell.——

Gall. Till then a thoufand times adieu.—— [*Blowing up kiffes to her.*

Phil. Ah Madam we're undone,——yonders *Crapine* your Uncles
Vallet.——

Cor. Now a curfe on him ; fhall we not have one Night with our
Cavaliers——let's retire, and continue to out-wit him, or never more
pretend to't, Adieu Signior Cavalier——remember Night.——

Gall. Or may I lofe my fenfe to all Eternity.
[*Kiffes his fingers and bows, fhe returns it for a while.*

Lau. Gods, that all this that looks at leaft like Love,
Shou'd be difpenc't to one infenfible !
Whilft every fillable of that dear vallue,
Whifper'd to me, wou'd make my foul all Extafy,
——Oh fpare that Treafure for a gratefull purchafe ;
And buy that common ware with trading Gold,
Love! is too rich a price :——I fhall betray my felf.—— [*Afide.*

Gall. Away, that's an hereticial opinion and which this certain
Reafon muft convince thee of:
That Love is Love, where ever beauty is,
Nor can the Name of whore, make beauty lefs.
Enter Marcella *like a Man, with a Cloak about her.*

Mar. Signior, is your Name *Fillamour* ?

Fill. It is, what wou'd you Sir.——

Mar. I have a letter for you——from *Vitterbo,*and your *Marcella* Sir.
[*gives it him*

Fill. Hah——*Vitterbo*! and *Marcella* !
It fhocks me like the Ghoft of fome forfaken Miftrefs,
That met me in the way to happinefs,
With fome new long'd for Beauty ! [*Opens it, reads.*

Mar. Now I fhall try thy Virtue, and my Fate.—— [*Afide.*

Fill. What is't that checks the joy, that fhou'd furprize me at the
receipt of this !

Gall. How now! what's the cold fit coming on ? [*Paufes.*

Fill. I have no power to go—where this——invites me——
By which I prove, 'tis no encreafe of flame that warms my heart,
But a new fire juft kindled from thofe——eyes——

Whofe

Whofe rayes I finde more piercing then *Marcella's*.

Gall. —Ay Gad a thoufand times——prethee what's the matter.

Mar. Oh this falfe——fouly man——wou'd I had leafure
To be reveng'd for this inconftancy !   [*Afide.*

Fill.—But ftill fhe want's that Virtue I admire !

Gall. Virtue ! s'death thou art always fumbling, upon that dull
ftring that makes no Mufick :——What Letters that ? [*reads.*] If the
firft Confeffion I ever made of Love be gratefull to you, come arm'd
to night with a friend or too ; and behinde the Garden of the Fountains, you will receive——hah *Marcella* !——Oh damn it, from your
honeft woman!——Well I fee the devil's never fo bufy with a man,
as when he has refolv'd upon any goodnefs ! s'death what a rubs here
in a fair caft,——how is't man - Alegremente ! bear up, defy him and
all's his works.

Fill. But I have fworn, fworn that I lov'd *Marcella* ! and Honour
Friend obliges me to go, take her away and marry her,
——And I conjure thee to affift me too.

Gall. What to night, this Night, that I have given to *Silvianetta* !
and you have promis'd to the fair—*Euphemia* !

Lau. If he fhou'd go, he ruins my defign,   [*Afide.*
——Nay if your word Sir——be already paft.——

Fill. 'Tis true, I gave my promife to *Euphemia* ! but that to women
of her trade, is eafily abfolv'd.

Gall. Men keep not Oaths for the fakes of the wife Magiftrates, to
whom they're made, but their own Honour *Harry*: And is't not much
a greater crime to Rob a Gallant, hofpitable man of his Neece, who
has treated you with Confidence, and Friendfhip, then to keep touch
with a well meaning whore, my Confciencious friend !

Lau. Iufinite degrees Sir !

Gall. Befides, thou'ft an hour or two good, between this and the
time requir'd to meet *Marcella.*

Lau. Which an induftrious Lover, wou'd manage to the beft advantage.

Gall. That were not given over to Virtue, and conftancy——two
the beft excufes I know for idleneffe.

Fill.——Yes—I may fee this woman.

Gall. Whe God a marcy lad !

Fill.——And break my chains,—if poffible.

Gall. Thou wilt give a good effay to that I'le warrant thee,
Before fhe part with thee ! come let's about it.
                      [*They go out on either fide of* Fill. *perfwading him.*

Mar. He's gone ! the Curtizan has got the day.   [*Afide to* Mar.
Vice has the ftart of Virtue, every way,
And for one bleffing honeft wives obtain,
The happyer Miftrefs does a thoufand gain !

                                                                    That

I'le home——and practice, all their Art to prove,
That nothing is so cheaply gain'd as Love !   [*Exeunt.*
  Gall. Stay what farce is this,——prethee let's see a little. [*offering to go*

  [*Enter* Sir Signal, *Mr.* Tickletext, *with his Cloke ty'd*
     about him, a great Ink-horn ty'd at his Girdle, and a great Folio
     under his Arm, Petro *dreſt like an Antiquary.*

——How Now Mr. *Tickletext,* what dreſt as if you were going a Pil-
grimage to *Jeruſalem.*
  Tick. I make no ſuch prophane Journeys, Sir.
  Gall. But where have you been Mr. *Tickletext.*
  Sir Sig. Whe Sir, this moſt Reverend and Renowned Antiquary,
has been ſhowing us Monimental Rarities and Antiquities.
  Gall. 'Tis *Petro* that——Rogue !
  Fill.——But what Folio have you gotten there Sir, *Knox,* or *Cart-*
wright?
  Pet. Nay if he be got into that heap of Nonſenſe, I'le ſteal oft and
undreſs.   [*Aſide.*   [*Ex.* Petro.   [Tick. *Opening the Book.*

  Tick. A ſmall Vollum Sir, into which I tranſcribe the moſt memorable
and remarkable tranſactions of the day.
  Lau. That doubtleſs muſt be worth ſeeing.

  Fill. [*Reads*] April the Twentieth, aroſe a very great ſtorm of
Wind, Thunder, Lightning, and Rain,——which was a ſhrew'd ſign
of foul weather.
  Fill. The 22th. 9 of our 12 chikens getting looſe, flew over-bord,
the other three miraculous eſcaping, by being eaten by me, that Morning for breakfaſt.
  Sir Sig. Harkey *Galliard*——thou art my Friend, and 'tis not like a
man of Honour, to conceal any thing from on's Friend,——know then I
am the moſt fortunate Raſcall, that ever broke bread,——I am this
Night to viſit ſirra—the fineſt, the moſt delicious young Harlot, Mum
——under the Roſe——in all *Rome* ! of *Barberacho's* acquaintance.
  Gall.——Hah——my woman on my life ! and will ſhe be kind !
  Sir Sig. Kind, hang kindneſſe man, I'me reſolv'd upon conqueſt by
parly or by force.
  Gall. Spoke like a Roman of the firſt Race, when Noble Rapes not
whining Courtſhip, did the Lovers buſineſs.
  Sir Sig. Sha Rapes man ! I mean by force of mony, pure dint of
Gold faith and troth : for I have given 500 Crowns enterance already,
& Par Dios Baccus 'tis *tropo Caro*——*tropo Caro* Mr. *Galliard.*

  Gall. And what's this high priz'd Ladys Name Sir ?
  Sir Sig. La Silvianetta,——and Lodges on the *Corſo,* not far from St.
James's of the incurables——very well ſcituated in caſe diſaſter——hah.——
                                                              Gall.

Gall. Very well,——and did not your wife worship know, this *Silvianetta* was my Miftrefs?

Sir *Sig.* How! his Miftrefs! what a damn'd noddy was! to name her!

Gall. De ye hear fool! renounce me this woman inftantly, or I'le firft difcover it to your Governor, and then cut your throat Sir.

Sir *Sig.* Oh *Doux Ment*——dear *Galliard* ——Renounce her,——*Corpo demi* that I will foul and body if fhe belong to thee man.——

Gall. No more——look to't,——look you forget her Name——or but to think of her ——farewell———   [*Nods at him.*

Sir *Sig.* Fare well quoth ye——'tis well I had the Art of diffembling after all, here had been a fweet Broyl upon the Coaft elfe.——

Fill. Very well, I'le trouble my felf to reade no more, fince I know you'l be fo kinde to the world to make it publique?

Tick. At my return Sir, for the good of the Nation, I will Print it, and I think it will deferve it.

Lau. This is a precious Rogue, to make a Tutor of.

Fill. Yet thefe Mooncalfs, dare pretend to the breeding of our youth, and the time will come, I fear, when none fhall be reputed to travel like a man of quality, who has not the advantage of being impos'd upon, by one of thefe pedantique Novices, who inftructs the young heir, in what himfelf is moft profoundly ignorant of.

Gall. Come, 'tis dark and time for our defign,——your fervant Signiors.   [*Exeunt* Fill. Gall. *and* Lau.

Lau. I'le home, and watch the kind deceiving minute, that may conduct him by miftake to me.

Enter Petro, *like* Barberacho, *juſt as* Tick *and Sir* Sig. *are going out.*

Sir *Sig.* Oh *Barberacho*! we are undone! Oh the Diavillo take that Mafter you fent me.

Pet. Mafter, what Mafter?

Sir *Sig.* Whe Signior Morigorofo!

Pet. Mor——ofo——what fhou'd he be?

Sir *Sig.* A Civillity-Mafter he fhou'd have been, to have taught us good manners,——but the Cornuto cheated us moft damnably, and by a willing miftake taught us nothing in the world but wit.

Pet. Oh abominable knavery! whe what a kinde of man was he?——

Sir *Sig,* ——whe——much fuch another as your felf:——

Tick. Higher, Signior, higher!

Sir *Sig.* Aye fomewhat higher——but juft of his pitch.

Pet. Well Sir, and what of this man?

Sir *Sig.* Only pick't our pockets, that's all.

Tick. Yes, and cozen'd us of our Rings.

Sir *Sig.* Ay, and gave us Cackamarda Orangata for fnuff.

Tick. And his bleffing to boot when he had done.

Sir *Sig.* A veng'ance on't, I feel it ftill.

                                        Pet.

Pet. Whe this 'tis to do things of your own heads, for I fent no fuch Signior Morofo—but I'le fee what I can do to retrive 'm—I am now a little in hafte, farwell.——   [*Offers to go.* Tick. *goes out by him and jogs him.*

Tick. Remember to meet me—farewell *Barberacho.*

[*Goes out,* Sir Sig. *pulls him.*

Sir *Sig.* Barberacho—is the Lady ready?

Tick. Is your money ready?

Sir *Sig.* Whe now, tho I am threatned, and kill'd, and beaten, and kickt about, this intrigue I muft advance! [*afide*]——but doft think there's no danger?

Pet. What in a delicate young amorous Lady, Signior?

Sir *Sig.* No, No, mum, I don't much fear the Lady, but this fame mad fellow *Galliard*, I hear, has a kinde of a hankering after her—Now dare not I tell him what a difcovery I have made.   [*Afide.*

Pet. Let me alone to fecure you, meet me in the *Piatzo Defpagnia*, as foon as you can get your felf in order; where the two fools fhall meet, and prevent eithers coming.   [*Afide.*

Sir *Sig.* Enough,——here's a Bill for 500 Crowns more upon my Merchant, you know him by a good token, I loft the laft fum you re-ceiv'd for me, a pox of that handfell, away here's company.

Ex. Pet. *Enter* Octavio.

Now will I difguife my felf, according to the mode of the Roman Ina-morato's; and deliver my felf upon the place appointed. [*Ex.*Sir Sig.

Oct. On the *Corfo* didft thou fee 'em?

Crap. On the *Corfo* my Lord, in difcourfe with three Cavaliers, one of which has given me many a Piftol, to let him into the Garden a Nights at *Viterbo*: to talk with *Dona Marcella*, from her Chamber window, I think I fhou'd remember him.

Oct. Oh that thought fires me, with anger fit for my Revenge, [*Afide.* And they're to Serinade 'em thou fay'ft.

Crap. I did my Lord! and if you can have patience till they come, you will finde your Rival in this very place, if he keep his word.

Oct. I do believe thee, and have prepared my Bravos to attack him: if I can Act but my Revenge to Night, how fhall I worfhip Fortune! keep out of fight, and when I give the word be ready all. I hear fome coming let's walk off a little.——

[*Enter* Marcella *in mans clothes, and* Philipa *as a woman, with a Lanthorn* Oct. *and* Crap. *go off the other way.*

Mar. Thou canft never convince me, but if *Crapine* faw us, and gaz'd fo long upon us, he muft know us too, and then what hin-ders but by a dilligent watch about the Houfe, they will furprize us, ere we have fecured our felves from 'em.

Phil. And how will this, expofing your felf to danger prevent 'em.

F   *Mar.*

Mar. My designe now is, to prevent *Fillamour* coming into danger, by hindring his approach to this house : I wou'd preserve the kinde ingrate with any hazard of my own : and 'tis better to dye then fall into the hands of *Octavio.* I'me desperate with that thought, ——and fear no danger ! however be you ready at the door, and when I ring admit me. ——ha——who comes here.——

[*Enter* Tickletext *with a Periwig and Cravat of Sir* Signals : *A Sword by his side, and a dark Lanthorn, she opens hers, looks on him and goes out.*

Tick. A man ! now am I though an old sinner, as timerous as a young thief, 'tis a great inconvenience in these Popish Countrys, that a man cannot have liberty to steal to a wench without danger ; not that I need fear who sees me except *Galliard,* who suspecting my business, will go neer to think I am wickedly inclin'd, Sir *Signal* I have left hard at his study, and Sir *Henry* is no Nocturnal Inamorato, unless like me he dissemble it,——well *Certo* 'tis a wonderfull pleasure to deceive the World : And as a learned man well observ'd, that *the sin of wenching lay in the habit only* : I having laid that aside, *Timothy Tickletext* principal holder forth of the *Covent Garden* Conventicle, Chaplain of *Buffoon-Hall* in the County of *Kent,* is free to recreate himself.

[*Enter* Gall. *with a dark Lanthorn.*

Gall. Where the devil is this *Fillamour* ? And the Musick : which way cou'd he go to lose me thus !   [*Looks towards the door.* ——he is not yet come.——

Tick. Not yet come,——that must be *Barberacho* !——where are ye honest *Barberacho* where are ye ?   [*Groping towards* Gall.

Gall. Hah ! *Barberach* ? that name I am sure is us'd by none but Sir *Signal* and his Coxcomb Tutor, it must be one of those——where are ye Signior, where are ye ?   [*Goes towards him, and opens the Lanthorn——and shuts it straight.* ——Oh 'tis the Knight,——are you there Signior ?

Tick. Oh art thou come, honest Rascal——conduct me quickly, conduct me to the Beautifull and fair *Silvianetta* !   [*Gives him his hand.*

Gall. Yes, when your dogships damn'd, *Silvianetta* ! S'death is she a whore for fools !   [*Draws.*

Tick. Hah Mr. *Galliard,* as the devil wou'd have it :——I'me undone if he sees me !   [*He retires hastily,* Gall. *gropes for him.*

Gall. Where are you Fop : *Buffoon* ! Knight !

[Tickletext *retiring hastily runs against* Octavio, *who is just entering, almost beats him down,* Oct. *strikes him a good blow, beats him back and draws :* Tick. *gets close up in a corner of the stage,* Oct. *gropes for him as* Gall. *does, and both meet and fight with each other.*

——What dare you draw,——you have the impudence to be valliant then

then in the dark, [*they pass*] I wou'd not kill the Rogue,——death you can fight then, when there's a woman in the cafe?

Oct. I hope 'tis *Fillamour*! [*aside*] you'le finde I can, and poffibly may fpoil your making love to Night!

Gall. Egad fweet heart and that may be, one civil thruft will do't:——And 'twere a damn'd rude thing to difappoint fo fine a woman,——therefore I'le withdraw whilft I'me well. [*He flips out.*

[*Enter* Sir Signal, *with a Mafquerading Coat over his clothes, with-out a Wigg or Cravat, with a dark Lanthorn.*

S*r* S*i.* Well! I have moft neatly efcapt my Tutor; and in this dif-guife defy the devil to claim his own,——ah *Cafpeto de Deavilo*!——What's that? [*Advancing foftly, and groping with his hands, meets the point of* O*ct.* *fword, as he is groping for* Gall.

Oct. Traytor dareft thou not ftand my fword!

Sir *Sig.* Hah! fwords! no Signior—*fcufa mea* Signior,——

[*Hops to the door:* *And feeling for his way with his out-ftrecht Arms, runs his Lanthorn in* Julio's *face who is juft entering; finds he's oppos'd with a good pufh backward, and flips afide into a corner over againft* Tickletext: Julio *meets* Octavio *and fights him,* Oct. *falls,* Julio *opens his Lanthorn and fees his miftake.*

Jul. Is it you Sir?

Oct. *Julio!* from what miftake grew all this violence?

Jul. That I fhou'd ask of you, who meet you arm'd againft me.

Oct. I find the Night has equally deceiv'd us; and you are fitly come! to fhare with me the hopes of dear Revenge!

[*Gropes for his Lanthorn which is dropt.*

Jul. I'de rather have purfu'd my kinder paffion!

Love! and defire! that brought me forth to Night!

Oct. I've learnt where my falfe Rival is to be this Evening,

And if you'l joyn your fword, you'l finde it well imploy'd.

Jul. Lead on, I'me as impatient of Revenge as you.——

Oct. Come this way then, you'l find more aids to ferve us. [*Go out.*

Tick.——So! thanks be prais'd all's ftill again, this fright were e-nough to mortify any Lover of lefs magnanimity then my felf,——well of all fins, this itch of whoring is the moft hardy,——the moft impu-dent in repulfes; the moft vigilant in watching, moft patient in wait-ing, moft frequent in dangers: in all difafters but difappointment, a Philofopher! yet if *Barberacho* come not quickly, my Philofophy will be put to't *certo.* [*This while Sir* Signal *is venturing from his poft, liftening and flowly advancing towards the middle of the ftage.*

Sir *Sig.* The coaft is once more clear, and *I* may venture my carcafs forth again,——though fuch a falutation as the laft, wou'd make me very unfit for the matter in hand,——the battoon I cou'd bear with the

Fortitude and courage of *Hero* : But these dangerous sharps *I* never lov'd; what different rancounters have *I* met withall to Night, *Corpo de me* ; a man may more safely pass the gulf of lyons, then convoy himself into a Bawdy house in *Rome*, but *I* hope all's past, and *I* will say with *Alexander* :——*Vivat Esperance en despetto del Fatto.*　　[*advances a little.*

Tick. Sure I heard a Noise,——No 'twas only my surmise !

> [*They both advance softly, meeting just in the middle of the Stage, and coming close up to each other ! both cautiously start back : And stand a tipto in the posture of fear, then gently feeling for each other, (after listening and hearing no noise) draw back their hands at touching each others ; and shrinking up their shoulders, make grimaces of more fear !*

Tick. Que Equesto.

Sir Sig. Hah a mans voice !——I'le try if I can fright him hence! [*Aside.* Una Malladette Spirito Incarnate !　　　　　　　　　[*In a horrible tone.*

Tick. Hah, *Spiritto Incarnate*! that devils voice I shou'd know ! [*aside.*

Sir Sig. See Signior ! *Una spirito* ! which is to say *un spiritalo, Imortallo Incorporalla, Inanimate, Imaterialle, Philosophicale, Invisible——Un intelligible——Diavillo* !　　　　　　　　　　　[*In the same tone.*

Tick. Ay ay, 'tis my hopefull pupill ! upon the same design with me, my life on't,——Cunning young whoremaster ! ——I'le cool your courage——good Signior *Diavillo* ! if you be the *Diavillo* I have *una certaina Imaterialle Invisible Conjuratione*, that will so neatly lay your *Inanimate unintelligible Diavilloship.*——　　　　　[*Pulls out his wooden sword.*

Sir Sig. How ! he must needs be valliant indeed that dares fight with the devil.　　　[*Endeavours to get away,* Tick. *beats him about the stage.* ——Ah Signior Signior *Mia* ! ah——*Caspeto de Baccus,*——he cornuto, I am a damn'd silly devil that have no dexterity in vanishing.

> [*Gropes and finds the door——going out, meets just entring* Fillamour Galliard *with all the Musick,——he retires and stands close.*

——Hah,——what have we here new mischief.——

> [Tick. *and he stands against each other, on either side of the stage.*

Fill. Prethee how came we to lose ye ?

Gall. I thought I had follow'd ye,——but 'tis well we are met again, come tune your pipes,——　[*They play a little,* Enter Marcella *as before.*

Mar. This must be he.　　　　　　　　　　[*Goes up to 'em.*

Gall. Come come, your Song boy your Song.

> [*Whilst 'tis singing Enter* Octavio, Julio, Crapine, *and* Bravo's !

The

The SONG.

Crudo Amore, Crudo Amore, } bis.
Il mio Core non fa per te
Suffrir non vo tormenti
Senza mai sperar mar ce
Belta che sia Tiranna,
Bolta che sia Tiranna
Dell meo offetto recetto non e
Il tuo rigor singunna
  Se le pene
  Le catene
Tenta auolgere al mio pie
See see Crudel Amore } bis.
Il mio Core non fa per te.

Lusinghiero, Lusinghiero, } bis.
Pui non Credo alta tua fe
L'incendio del tuo foce
Nel mio Core pui viuo none
Belta che li die Luoce
Belta che li die Luoce
Ma il rigor L'Ardore s'bande
Io non sato tuo gioce
  Cò il Veleno
  Del mio seno
Vergoroso faggito se n'e.
See see Crudel Amore } bis.
Il mio Core non fa per te.

Oct. 'Tis they we look for, draw and be ready.———
Tick. Hah draw——then there's no safty here *certo.* 　　　　[*Aside.*

[Octavio Julio *and their party draw, and fight with* Fill. *and* Gall.
Marcella *ingages on their side, all fight, the Musick confusedly a-
mongst 'em; Gall. loses his sword, and in the hurry gets a
Base Viol, and happens to strike* Tickletext, *who is getting away——
his head breaks its way quite through, and it hangs about his neck;
they fight out.*

Enter Petro *with a Lanthorn. Sir* Signal *stands close still.*
Tick. Oh undone, undone, where am I, where am I.
Pet. Hah——that's the voice of my Amorous Ananias,——or I am
mistaken——what the devil's the matter. 　　　[*Opens his Lanthorn.*
——Where are ye Sir,——hah cuts so——what new found pillory have
we here.?

Tick.

Tick. Oh honeſt *Barberacho* undo me, undo me quickly.

Pet. So I deſign Sir, as faſt as I can——or loſe my aim——there Sir there: all's well——I have ſet you free, come follow me the back way, into the houſe.   [*Ex.* Petro *and* Tickletext.

Enter Fillamour *and* Marcella, *with their ſwords drawn* Gall. *after 'em.*

Gall. A plague upon 'em, what a quarters here for a wench, as if there were no more i'th Nation,——wou'd I'de my ſword again.
                                                  [*Gropes for it.*

Mar. Which way ſhall I direct him to be ſafer,——how is it Sir, I hope you are not hurt.

Fill. Not that I feel, what art thou asks't ſo kindly.

Mar. A ſervant to the Roman Curtizan, who ſent me forth to wait your coming Sir, but finding you in danger ſhar'd it with you,—— come let me lead you into ſafety Sir.——

Fill. Thou'lt been too kinde to give me cauſe to doubt thee.

Mar. Follow me Sir, this key will give us entrance through the Garden.   [*Exeunt.*

Enter Octavio *with his ſword in his hand.*

Oct. ! Oh what damn'd luck had I ſo poorly to be vanquiſh't when all is huſht, I know he will return,——therefore I'le fix me here, till I become a furious ſtatue——but I'le reach his heart.

Sir Sig. Oh *lamentivolo fato*——What bloody Villains theſe Popiſh Itallians are.

Enter Julio.

Oct. Hah——*I* hear one coming this way—— ——hah——the door opens too,——and he makes towards it—pray Heaven he be the right : for this *I*'me ſure's the Houſe? ——Now luck an't be thy will,——[*Follows* Julio *towards the door ſoftly.*

Jul. The Rogues are fled but how ſecure *I* know not,—— And *I*'le purſue my firſt deſign of Love, And if this *Silvianetta* will be kind.——

          [*Enter* Laura *from the houſe in a Night gown.*

Lau. Whi'ſt——who is't Names *Silvianetta?*

Jul. A Lover and her ſlave.——   [*She takes him by the hand.*

Lau. Oh is it you,——are you eſcapt unhurt ? Come to my boſome——and be ſafe for ever——

Jul. 'Tis Love that calls, and now Revenge muſt ſtay,——this hour is thine fond Boy, the next that is my own *I*'le give to anger.——

Oct. Oh ye pernicious pair,——I'le quickly change the Scene of Love into a ruffer and more unexpected entertainment.

                                                  [*She*

[*She leads* Julio *in,*——Oct. *follows close, they shut the door upon 'em.*
Sir Sig. *thrusts out his head to hearken, hears no body and advances.*

Sir Sig. Sure the devil raigns to Night, wou'd I were shelter'd and let him raign fire and Brimstone, for pass the streets I dare not——this shou'd be the house——or here abouts I'me sure 'tis,——hah——what's this——a string——of a Bell I hope——I'le try to enter ; and if I am mistaken 'tis but crying con[licentia!   [*Rings Enter* Philipa.

Phil. Whose there ?

Sir Sig. 'Tis I, 'tis I, let me in quickly.——

Phil. Who——the English Cavalier.

Sir Sig. The same——I am right——I see I was expected.

Phil. I'me glad you're come,——give me your hand.——

Sir Sig. I am fortunate at last,——and therefore will say with the Famous Poet.

——No happiness like that achiv'd with danger,
Which once o'recome——i'le ly at Rack and Manger.   [*Exeunt.*

ACT IV. SCENE I.

Enter Fillamour *and* Galliard, *as in* Silvianetta's *apartment.*

Fill.——How splendidly these Common women live,
How rich is all we meet with in this Palace,
And rather seems th' Apartment of some Prince,
Then a Receptickle for lust and shame.

Gall. You see *Harry,* all the keeping fools are not in our dominions but this grave this wife people, are Mistress riden too.

Fill. I fear we have mistook the house, and the youth that brought us in may have deceived us, on some other design, however whilst I've this—— cannot fear.——   [*Draws.*

Gall. A good caution, and I le stand upon my guard with this, but see——here's one will put us out of doubt. [*Pulls a pistol out of his pocket.*

Fill. Hah! the fair Inchantress !   [*Enter* Mar. *richly and loosly drest.*

Mar. What on your guard my lovely Cavalier ! lyes there a danger In this Face and Eyes, that needs that rough resistance ?
——Hide hide that mark of anger from my sight,
And if thou woud'st be absolute conqueror here,
Put on soft looks with Eyes all languishing,
Words tender, gentle sighs, and kind desires.

Gall. Death ! with what unconcern he hears all this ? art thou possest——pox why dost not answer her?

Mar. I hope he will not yield,——   [*Afide.*
—He ftands unmov'd,——
Surely I was miftaken in this face,
And I believe in charms that have no power.

Gall. S'death thou deferveft not fuch a Noble creature,——
I'le have 'em both my felf.——   [*Afide.*

Fill.—Yes! thou haft wonderous power,
And I have felt it long.   [*Pawfingly.*

Mar. How!

Gall.—I've often feen that face—but 'twas in dreams:
And fleeping lov'd Extreamly!
And waking—figh't to find it but a dream,
The lovely Phantom vanifh't with my flumbers,
But left a ftrong *Idea* on my heart;
Of what I finde in perfect Beauty here,
—But with this difference, fhe was Virtuous too!

Mar. What filly fhe was that!

Fill. She whom I dream't I Lov'd.

Mar. You only dream't that fhe was Virtuous too!
Virtue it felf's a dream of fo flight force,
The very fluttering of Loves wings deftroys it,
Ambition, or the meaner hope of intereft, wakes it to nothing,
In men a feeble Beauty, fhakes the dull flumber off,——

Gall. Egad fhe argues like an Angell *Harry*!

Fill.——What haft thou'ft made, to damn thy felf fo young!
Haft thou been long thus wicked? haft thou fin'd paft Repentance,
Heaven may do much, to fave fo fair a Criminal,
Turn yet and be forgiven!

Gall. What a pox doft thou mean by all this canting?

Mar. A very pretty Sermon, and from a prieft fo gay,
It cannot chufe but edify.
Do Holy men of your Religion Signior, wear all this Habit,
Are they thus young, and lovely? fure if they are,
Your Congregation's all compos'd of Ladys,
The Layety muft come abroad for Miftreffes.

Fill. Oh that this charming woman were but honeft!

Gall. 'T were better thou wer't damn'd; honeft!
Pox thou doft come out with things fo malapropo——

Mar. Come leave this Mask of foolifh modefty,
And let us haft where Love and Mufick call's;
Mufick! that heightens Love! and makes the foul,
Ready for foft impreffions!

Gall. So, fhe will do his bufinefs with a Vengeance!

Fill. Plague of this tempting woman fhe will ruin me!
I finde weak Virtue melt from round my heart,

                                                To

To give her Tyrant Image a Poſſeſſion :
So the warm Sun, thaws Rivers Icy tops,

Till in the ſtream he ſees his own bright face !

Gall. Now he comes on apace,——how is't my friend,
Thou ſtand ſt as thou'dſt forgot thy buſineſs here !
——The woman *Harry* ! the fair Curtizan !
Canſt thou withſtand her charms ? I've buſineſs of my own,
Prethee fall too——and talk of Love to her.

Fill. Oh I cou'd talk Eternity away,
In nothing elſe but Love !——cou'dſt thou be honeſt ?

Mar. Honeſt ! was it for that you ſent two thouſand Crowns.
Or did believe that trifling ſum ſufficient,
To buy me to the ſlavery of honeſty.

Gall. Hold there my brave Virago.

Fill. No, I wou'd ſacrifice a Nobler Fortune,
To buy thy Virtue home !

Mar. What ſhou'd it idling there !

Fill. Whe——make thee conſtant to ſome happy man,
That wou'd adore thee for't.

Mar. Unconſcionable ! conſtant at my years ?
——Oh t'were to cheat a thouſand !
Who between this and my dull Age of Conſtancy,
Expect the diſtribution of my Beauty.

Gall. 'Tis a brave wench,——   [*Aſide.*

Fill. Yet charming as thou art, the time will come
When all that Beauty like declining flowers,
Will wither on the ſtalk,——but with this difference,
The next kinde Spring, brings youth to flowers again,
But faded Beauty never more can bloom,
——If intreſt make thee wicked, I can ſupply thy pride.——

Mar. Curſe on your neceſſary traſh !——which I deſpiſe, but as 'tis
uſefull to advance our Love !

Fill. Is Love thy buſineſs, who is there born ſo high,
But Love and Beauty equals ,
And thou maiſt chuſe from all the wiſhing world ?
This wealth together wou'd inrich one man,
Which dealt to all wou'd ſcarce be Charity.

Mar. Together ! 'tis a Maſs wou'd Ranſome King's !
Was all this Beauty given, for one poor petty Conqueſt ;
——I might have made a hundred hearts my ſlaves,
In this loſt time of bringing one to Reaſon.——
Farewell thou dull Philoſopher in Love ;
When Age has made me wiſe,——I'le ſend for you again.

         [*Offers to go Gall. holds her.*

Gall. By this good light a Noble glorious Whore!

Fill. Oh stay,——I muſt not let ſuch Beauty fall,
——A whore——conſider yet, the charms of Reputation:
The eaſe, the quiet and content of innocence,
The awfull Reverence, all good men will pay thee,
Who as thou art will gaze without reſpect,
——And cry——what pitty 'tis ſhe is——a whore——

Mar. O you may give it what courſe Name you pleaſe;
But all this youth and Beauty ne're was given,
Like Gold to Miſers, to be kept from uſe.   [*Going out.*

Fill. Loſt loſt,——paſt all Redemption.

Gall. Nay, Gad thou ſhalt not loſe her ſo,——I'le fetch her back,
And thou ſhalt ask her pardon.   [*Runs out after her.*

Fill. By Heaven 'twas all a dream! an Aiery dream!
The Viſionary pleaſure diſappears,——and I'me my ſelf again,
—— 'le fly, before the drowſy fit ore'take me.
    [*Going out, Enter* Gall. *and then* Marcella.

Gall. Turn back——ſhe yields, ſhe yields to pardon thee,——gon——
Nay hang me if ye part.   [*Runs after him, ſtill his Piſtol in his hand.*

Mar. Gon——I have no leaſure now for more diſſembling.
    [*Takes the Candle and goes in.*

Enter Petro, *leading in Mr.* Tickletext, *as by dark.*

Pet. Remain here Signior whilſt I ſtep and fetch a light.

Tick. Do ſo, do ſo honeſt *Barberacho!*——well my eſcape even now from Sir *Signal* was Miraculous! thanks to my prudence and proweſs, had he diſcover'd me, my dominion had ended; and my Authority been of non effect *certo.*   [Philipa *at the door puts in Sir* Signal.

Phil. Now Signior yo're out of danger, I'le fetch a Candle; and let my Lady know of your being here.   [*Ex.* Phil.
    [*Sir* Sig. *advances a little.*

Enter Petro *with a light, goes between 'em and ſtarts.*

Tick. Sir *Signal!*——

Sir *Sig.* My Governor!

Pet. The two fools met! a pox of all ill luck: now ſhall I loſe my credit with both my wiſe Patrons, my Knight I cou'd have put off, with a ſmall Harlot of my own, but my Levite having ſeen my Lady *Cornelia* that is *La Silvianetta,*——None but that *Suſanna* wou'd ſatisfy his Elder-ſhip: but now they have both ſav'd me the labour of a farther inventi-on to diſpatch 'em.

Sir *Sig.* I perceive my Governor's as much confounded as my ſelf; ——I'le take advantage by the forelock, be very impudent and put it upon him faith.——Ah Governor, will you never leave your whoring! never be ſtayd, ſober and diſcreet as I am.

Tick. So fo, undone undone, juſt my Documents to him.——

[*Walks about,* Sir Sig. *follows.*

Sir *Sig.* And muſt I neglect my pretious ſtudys, to follow you, in pure zeal and tender care of your perſon ! will you never conſider where you are ? in a lewd Papiſh Country ! amongſt the Romiſh Heathens,——and for you a Governor, a Tutor, a director of unbridled youth, a Gown-man, a Polititian, for you I ſay to be taken at this unrighteous time of the Night, in a flaunting Cavaliero dreſs, an unlawful weapon by your ſide, going the high way to Satan to a Curtizan ! and to a Romiſh Curtizan ! Oh abomination, Oh *ſcandalum infiniti.*

Tick. Paid in my own Coyn !

Pet. So, I'le leave the devil to rebuke ſin, and to my young Lady, for a little of her aſſiſtance, in the management of this affair.

[*Exit.* Pet. Tick.

Tick.——I do confeſs,——I grant ye I am in the houſe of a Curtizan, and that I came to viſit a Curtizan, and do intend to viſit each Night a ſeveral Curtizan :——till I have finiſht my work.——

Sir *Sig.* Every Night one ! Oh glutton !

Tick.——My great work of Converſion,——upon the whole Nation, Generation, and Vocation, of this wicked provoking ſort of womankinde ; call'd Curtizans :——I will turn 'em——yes I will turn 'em,——for 'tis a ſhame that Man——ſhou'd bow down to thoſe that worſhip Idols ! ——and now I think Sir, I have ſufficiently explain'd the buſineſs in hand,——as honeſt *Barberacho* is my witneſs !——And for you——to—— ſcandalize——me——with ſo naughty an interpretation——afflicteth me wonderfully.——   [*Pulls out his hankerchief and weeps.*

Sir *Sig.*——Alas poor Mr. *Tickletext,* now as I hope to be ſav'd it grieves my heart to ſee him weep,——faith and troth now, I thought thou had'ſt ſome Carnal aſſignation,——but nere ſtir I beg thy pardon and think thee as innocent as my ſelf, that I do——but ſee the Ladys, here——s'life dry your Eyes man !   [*Enter* Cornelia Phil. *and* Pet.

Cor. I cou'd beat thee for being thus miſtaken,——and am reſolv'd to flatter him into ſome miſchief, to be Reveng'd on 'em for this diſappointment, go you and watch for my Cavalier the while.

Tick. Is ſhe come——Nay then turn me looſe to her.——

Cor. My Cavalier ! [*Addreſſing to Sir* Sig. Tick. *pulls him by and ſpeaks.*

Tick.——Lady.——

Sir *Sig.* You Sir, whe who the devil made you a Cavalier,——moſt *Potentiſimo Signiora,* I am the man of Title, by Name Sir *Signal Buffoon,* ſole Son and heir to Eight Thouſand pound a year.——

Tick. Oh Sir, are you the man ſhe looks for ?

Sir *Sig.* I Sir, No Sir, I'de have ye to know Sir, I ſcorn any woman be ſhe never ſo fair, unleſs her deſigne be honeſt and Honourable !

Cor. The man of all the World I've choſen out, from all the wits and Beauties I have ſeen ;——to have moſt finely beaten !

G 2   Sir *Sig.*

Sir Sig. How! in Love with me already,——she's damnable handsome too, now wou'd my Tutor were hang'd a little for an hour or two,
out of the way.   [*Aside.*

Cor. Why fly you not into my Arms,   [*she approching, he shuning:*
These Arms that were defign'd for foft embraces?

Sir Sig. Ay, and if my Tutor were not here, the devil take him
that wou'd hinder 'em,——and I think that's civil egad!

Tick. Whe how now *Barberacho,* what am I cuzend then, and is Sir
Signal the Man in favour!   -   [*Aside to* Petro.

Pet. Lord Signior, that fo wife a man as you cannot perceive her
meaning ;   forthe devil take me if I can,——[*Aside.*]——Whe this
is done to take off all fufpition from you ——and lay it on him;——don't
you conceive it Signior!

Tick. Yes honeft Rogue,——Oh the witty wagtail,——*I* have a part
to play too, that fhall confirm it——young Gentlewoman.——

Cor. Ah bell ingrate, is't thus you recompence my fuffering Love?
to fly this beauty fo ador'd by all, that flight the ready conqueft of the
world to truft a heart with you,——ah—Traditor Cruella.

Sir Sig. Poor heart, it goes to the very foul of me to be fo coy and
fcornfull to her that it does, but a pox on't her over-fondnefs will difcover all.

Tick. Fly, fly, young man! whilft yet thou haft a fpark of virtue
fhining in thee, fly the temptations of this young hypocrite; the love
that fhe pretends with fo much zeal and ardour , is indecent, unwarrantable, and unlawful! firft indecent as fhe is woman——for thou art
woman——and beautiful woman——yes, very beautifull woman! on
whom nature hath fhew'd her heighth of excellence in the out-work,
but left the in unfinifht, imperfect and impure.

Cor. Heavens, what have we here *!*

Sir Sig. A pox of my Sir *Dominie,* Now is he befide his Text, and
will fpoil all.

Tick. Secondly, Unwarrantable ; by what authority doft thou feduce
with the allurements of thine eyes, and the conjurements of thy tongue,
the waftings of thy hands, and the tinklings of thy feet, the young
men in the Villages ?

Cor. Sirrah! how got this madman in? feize him, and take him
hence.

Sir Sig. Corpo de mi my Governour tickles her notably i'faith——but
had he let the care of my foul alone to night, and have let me taken
care of my body, 'twould have been more material at this time.

Tick. Thirdly, Unlawful——.

Cor. Quite diftracted! in pity take him hence, and leade him into
darkneffe, 'twill fute his madnefs beft.

                                                      Tick.

Tick. How, diſtracted! take him hence !

Pet. This was lucky——I knew ſhe wou'd come again——take him hence——yes, into her bed-chamber——pretty device to get you to her ſelf Signior.

Tick. Why but is it——nay, then I will facillitate my departure—— therefore I ſay——oh moſt beautifull and tempting woman——

[Beginning to preach again.

Cor. Away with him, give him clean ſtraw and darkneſſe, And chain him faſt for fear of further miſchief.

Pet. She means for fear of loſing ye.

Tick. Ah baggage! as faſt as ſhe will in thoſe pretty arms,

[Going to leade him off.

Sir. Sig. Hold, hold man, Mad ſaid ye——ha, ha, ha——mad ! whe we have a thouſand of theſe in *England* that go looſe about the ſtreets, and paſs with us for as ſober diſcreet religious perſons—— As a man ſhall wiſh to talk nonſenſe withall.

Pet.——You are miſtaken Signior, I ſay he is mad ——ſtark mad,

Sir Sig. Prethee Barberacho what doſt thou mean——

Pet. To rid him hence that ſhe may be alone with you——'slife Sir, you're madder then he——don't you conceive——

Sir Sig. Ay, ay! nay, I confeſſe, Illuſtriſſima Signiora, my Gover-nour has a Fit that takes him now and then, a kinde of a frenzy,—— a figary——a whimſie——a maggot that bites always at naming of Po-pery :——ſo ——he's gone.——Belliſſimo Signiora,——you have moſt ar-tificially remov'd him——and this extraordinary proof of your affecti-on is a ſigne of ſome ſmall kindeneſſe towards me, and though I was ſomething coy and reſerv'd before my Governour , Excellentiſſimo, Signiora, let me tell you, your love is not caſt away.

Cor. Oh Sir you bleſſe too faſt ! but will you ever love me——

Sir Sig. Love thee! I and lie with thee too, Moſt Magnanimous Signiora, and beget a whole Race of Roman *Julius Cæſars* upon thee; nay, now we're alone, turn me looſe to impudence, i'faith.

[ruffles her, Enter Philipa *in haſte, ſhutting the door after her.*

Phil. Oh Madam here's the young mad Engliſh Cavalier got into the houſe, and will not be deny'd ſeeing you.

Cor. This was lucky !

Sir Sig. How the mad Engliſh Cavalier ! If this ſhou'd be our young Count *Galliard* now——I were in a ſweet taking——oh I know by my fears 'tis he ; oh prethee what kinde of a manner of man is he?

Phil. A handſome——reſolute——brave——bold——

Sir Sig. Oh enough enough——Madam——I'le take my leave——I ſee you are——ſomething buſie at preſent,——and I'le —

Cor. Not for the World,——*Philipa*—bring in the Cavalier——that you may ſee there's none here fears him Signior.

Sir

Sir Sig. Oh hold hold,—Madam you are miſtaken in that point, for to tell you the truth, I do fear,—having—a certain—averſion or Antipathy,—to—Madam—a Gentleman—whe Madam they're the very Monſters of the Nation, they devour every day a Virgin.—

Cor. Good Heavens ! and is he ſuch a Fury !

Sir Sig. Oh and the veryeſt Belzebub,—beſides Madam he vow'd my Death, if ever he catch me neer this houſe, and he ever keeps his word in caſes of this Nature,—Oh that's he,   [*Knocking at the door.* I know it by a certain trembling inſtinct about me,—Oh what ſhall I do.—

Cor. Whe—I know not,—can you leap a high window ?

Sir Sig.—He knocks again,—I proteſt I'me the worſt Vaulter in Chriſtendom,—have ye no moderate danger,—between the two ex- treams of the window or the mad Count ? no Cloſet,—fear has dwin- dl'd me to the ſcantling of a Mouſehole.

Cor.—Let me ſee,—I have no leaſure to purſue my Revenge farther, and will reſt ſatisfy'd with this,—for this time——   [*Aſide.* ——Give me the Candle,—and whilſt *Philipa* is conducting the Cava- lier to the *Alcove* by dark,—you may have an opportunity to ſlip out, ——perhaps there may be danger in his being ſeen,——   [*Aſide.* ——farewell fool.——   [*Ex.* Cornelia *with the Candle,* Phil. *goes to* *the door, lets in* Gall. *takes him by the hand.*

Gall. Pox on't my Knights bound for *Vitterbo,* and there's no per- ſwading him into ſafe harbour again,——he has given me but two hours to diſpatch matters here,——and then I'me to imbark with him upon this new diſcovery of honourable Love, as he calls it,   whoſe ad- venturers are fools, and the returning Cargo, that dead Commodity call'd a wife ! a Voyage very ſutable to my humour,——who's there ?——

Phil. A Slave of *Silvianetta's,* Sir give me your hand.——
     [*Ex. Over the ſtage. Sir Sig. goes out ſoftly.*

`[ The Scene changes to a Bed Chamber Alcove,` Petro *leading in* Tickletext.

Pet. Now Signior you're ſafe and happy; in the Bed-Chamber of your Miſtreſs.—who will be here immediately I'me ſure, I'le fetch a light and put you to bed in the mean time.——

Tick. Not before ſupper I hope honeſt *Barberacho* !

Pet. Oh Signior that you ſhall do lying, after the manner of the Ancient Romans.

Tick. Certo, and that was a marevllous good lazy cuſtome. [*Ex.* Pet.

     Enter Philipa *with* Galliard *by dark.*——

Phil. My Lady will be with you inſtantly.——   [*goes out.*
Tick. Hah, ſure I heard ſome body come ſoftly in at the door : I hope 'tis the young Gentlewoman !   [*He advances forward.*
     Gall.

Gall. Silence ! and Night ! Love and dear opportunity !
                         [*In a soft tone.*
Joyn all your aids to make my *Silvia* kinde,
For I am fild with the expecting blifs, [*Tick. thrufts his head out to liften.*
And much delay, or difappointment kills me.
  Tick. Difappointment kills me,——and me too *certo.*——'tis fhe.——
                           [*Gropes about.*
  Gall. Oh hafte my fair, hafte to my longing Arms,——
Where are you dear and lovely ft of your sex ?
  Tick. That's I, that's !, *mi Alma! mea core mea vita !* ——
                     [*Groping and fpeaking low.*

  Gall. Hah——art thou come my life ! my foul ! my joy !——
             [*Goes to embrace,* Tick. *they meet and kifs.*
——S'death what's this a bearded Miftrefs ! Lights lights there, quickly
lights, --Nay curfe me if thou fcap'ft me.---
         [Tick. *ftruggles to get away, he holds him by the Cravat and Peri-*
        wig, Enter Petro *with a Candle.*
  Gall. Barberacho,——confound him 'tis the fool ! whom I found this
Evening about the Houfe, hovering to rooft him here !---hah---what
the devil have I caught---a *Tarter ?* Efcap't again ! the devil's his con-
federate.---
                           [*Groping.*
         [Pet. *puts out the Candle, comes to* Tick. *unties his Cravat behind,*
        and he flips his head out of the Periwig and gets away, leaving both
        in Gall.*'s hands.*

  Pet. Give me your hand, I'le leade you a back pair of ftairs through
the Garden.
  Tick. Oh any way to fave my Reputation——oh——
  Gall. Let me but once more grafp thee, and thou fhalt finde more
fafety in the Devils clutches ! none but my Miftrefs ferve ye.
                     [*Gropes out after him.*
  [Pet. *with* Tick. *running over the ftage,* Gall. *after'em, with the Cravat*
and Perewig in one hand, his Piftol in t'other.

                 Enter Philipa *with a light.*

  Phil. Mercy upon us, what's the matter——what noife is this—hah
a Piftol---what can this mean ?   [*A Piftol goes off.*
                  Enter Sir Signal. *running.*

  Sir Sig. Oh fave me, gentle devil, fave me, the ftairs are fortify'd
witk Canons and double Culverins ; I'me purfu'd by a whole Regiment
of arm'd men ! here,s gold, gold in abundance ! fave me——
  Phil. What Canons ? what arm'd men ?
  Sir Sig. Finding my felf purfu'd as I was groping my way through
the Hall, and not being able to finde the door, I made towards the
                              ftairs.

ftairs again, at the foot of which I was faluted with a great gaun——
a pox of the courtefie.

Gall. [*Without*] Where are ye Knight, buffoon, dog of *Egypt* ?

Sir Sig. Thunder and Lightning ? 'tis *Galliards* voice——

Phil. Here, ftep behinde this hanging——there's a Chimney which
may fhelter ye till the ftorm be over,—if you be not fmother'd before.

[*Puts him behinde the Arras,----Enter* Gall. *as before,*
and Corn. *at the other door.*

Cor. Havens ! what rude noife is this ?

Gall. Where have you hid this fool, this lucky fool?
He whom blinde chance, and more ill-judging woman
Has rais'd to that degree of happineffe
That witty men muft figh and toyl in vain for.

Cor. Wat fool, what happineffe ?

Gall. Ceafe cunning falfe one to excufe thy felf,
See here the Trophees of your fhameful choice,
And of my ruine, cruel---fair---deceiver !

Cor. Deceiver Sir, of whom——in what defpairing minute did I
fwear to be a conftant Miftrefs ? to what dull whining Lover did I vow
and had the heart to break it.

Gall. Or if thou hadft, I know of no fuch dog as wou'd believe
thee; no, thou art falfe to thy own charms, and haft betray'd 'em
To the poffeffion of the vileft wretch
That ever Fortune curft with happinefs;
Falfe to thy joys, falfe to thy wit and youth
All which thou'ft damn'd with fo much careful induftry
To an eternal fool,
That all the arts of love can ne're redeem thee !

Sir Sig. Meaning me, meaning me :   [*Peeping out of the Chimny*
his face blackt.

Cor. A fool, what indifcretion have you feen in me, fhou'd make ye
think I wou'd choofe a witty man for a lover, who perhaps loves out
his moneth in pure good husbandry, and in that time does more mifchief then a hundred fools; ye conquer without refiftance, ye treat
without pity, and triumph without mercy ; and when you're gone,
the world crys——fhe had not wit enough to keep him, when indeed
you are not fool enough to be kept ! thus we forfeit both our Liber-
ties and difcretion with you villanous witty men; for wifedom is but
good fuccefs in things, and thofe that fail are fools !

Gall. Moft glorioufly difputed !
You're grown a Machivillian in your Art.

Cor. Oh neceffary Maxims only, and the firft Politiques we learn
from obfervation —I've known a Curtezan grown infamous, defpis'd,
decay'd, and ruin'd, in the poffeffion of you witty men, who when fhe
had

had the luck to break her chains, and cast her net for fools, has liv'd in
state, finer then Brides upon their wedding-day, and more profuse then
the young amorous Coxcomb that set her up an idoll.

Sir Sig. Well argu'd of my side, I see the Bagage loves me!

                        [*Peeping out with a face more smutted.*

Gall. And hast thou! oh, but prethee Jilt me on,
And say thou hast not, destin'd all thy charms,
To such a wicked use;
Is that dear Face and Mouth for slaves to kiss:
Shall those bright Eyes be gaz'd upon, and serve
But to reflect the Images of fools?

Sir Sig. That's I still.   [*Peeping more black.*

Gall. Shall that soft tender bosome be approcht,
By one who wants a Soul, to breathe in languishment,
At every kiss that presses it.

Sir Sig. Soul, what a pox care I for Soul,——as long as my person
is so Amiable.——

Gall.——No, Renounce that dull discretion that undoes thee,
Cunning is cheaply to be wise, leave it to those that have
No other powers to gain a Conquest by,
It is below thy charms;——.
——Come swear,——and be forsworn most damnably,——
Thou hast not yielded yet; say 'twas intended only,
And though thou ly'st, by Heaven I must believe thee,——
——Say,——hast thou—given him—all?

Cor. I've done as bad, we have discourst th'affair,
And 'tis concluded on.——

Gall. As bad! by Heaven much worse! discours'd with him,
Were't thou so wretched, so depriv'd of sense,
To hold discourse with such an Animal?
Damn it! the sin is ne're to be forgiven!
——Had'st thou been wanton to that lewd degree,
By dark he might have been conducted to thee;
Where silently he might have serv'd thy purpose,
And thou had'st had some poor excuse for that!
But bartering words with fools admits of none.

 Cor. I grant ye,——had I talk't sense to him,——which had been enough
to have lost him for ever.

Sir Sig. Poor Devil, how fearfull 'tis of losing me!   [*Aside.*

Gall. That's some atonement for thy other sins,——come break thy
word and wash it quite away.

Sir Sig. That cogging won't do my good friend, that won't do.

Gall. Thou shalt be just and perjur'd, and pay my heart the debt of
Love you owe it.

 Cor. And wou'd you have the heart——to make a whore of me?

                      H   *Gall.*

Gall. With all my Soul, and the Devils in't if I can give thee a greater proof of my paſſion.

Cor. I rather fear you wou'd deboch me, into that dull ſlave call'd a wife:

Gall. A wife! have I no Conſcience, no Honour in me!
Prethee believe I wou'd not be ſo wicked,—
No,—my deſires are generous! and Noble,
To ſet thee up, that glorious inſolent thing,
That makes mankinde ſuch ſlaves! almighty Curtizan!
—Come! to thy private Chamber let us haſte,
The ſacred Temple of the God of Love!
And conſecrate thy power!   [*Offers to bear her off.*

Cor. Stay, do you take me then for what I ſeem!

Gall. I'me ſure I do! and wou'd not be miſtaken for a Kingdome!
But if thou art not! I can ſoon mend that fault,
And make thee ſo,—come—I'me impatient to begin the Experiment,
                                   [*Offers again to carry her off.*

Cor. Nay then I am in earneſt,—hold miſtaken ſtranger!—I am of
Noble birth! and ſhou'd I in one hapleſs loving minute, deſtroy the
Honour of my Houſe, ruin my youth and Beauty! and all that virtuous
Education, my hoping parents gave me?

Gall. Pretty diſſembl'd pride and innocence! and wounds no leſs
then ſmiles!—come let us in,—where I will give thee leave to frown
and Jilt, ſuch pretty frauds advance the appetite.   [*Offers again.*

Cor. By all that's good I am a Maid of Quality!
Bleſt with a Fortune equal to my Birth!

Gall. I do not credit thee, or if I did!
For once I wou'd diſpence with Quality,
And to expreſs my Love! take thee with all theſe faults!

Cor. And being ſo, can you expect I'le yield?

Gall. The ſooner for that Reaſon if thou'rt wiſe;
The Quality will take away the ſcandal,—
Do not torment me longer.—   [*Offers to lead her again.*

Cor. Stay and be undeceiv'd,—I do conjure ye.—

Gall. Art thou no Curtizan?

Cor. Not, on my life nor do intend to be!

Gall. No proſtitute! nor doſt intend to be?

Cor. By all that's good, I only feign'd to be ſo!

Gall. No Curtizan! haſt thou deceiv'd me then?
Tell me thou wicked—honeſt couzening Beauty!
Why did'ſt thou draw me in, with ſuch a fair pretence,
Why ſuch a temping preface to invite,
And the whole piece ſo uſeleſs and unedifying?
—Heavens! not a Curtizan!
Why from thy window did'ſt thou take my vows,

                                              And

And make fuch kinde returns? Oh damn your quality, what honeſt
Whore but wou'd have ſcorn'd thy cunning.

Cor. I make ye kinde returns!

Gall.—Perſwade me out of that too! 'twill be like thee!

Cor. By all my wiſhes I never held diſcourſe with you—but this Evening ſince I firſt ſaw your face!

Gall. Oh the Impudence of Honeſty and quallity in woman!
A plague upon 'em both, they have undone me,
Bear witneſs Oh thou gentle Queen of night,
Goddeſs of ſhades, ador'd by Lovers moſt;
How oft under thy covert ſhe has damn'd her ſelf,
With feigned love to me!   [*in paſſion.*

Cor. Heavens! this is Impudence, that power I call to witneſs too
how damnably thou injur'ſt me;   [*angry.*

Gall. You never from your Window talk't of love to me?

Cor. Never.

Gall. So, nor you're no Curtizan;

Cor. No by my life!

Gall. So, nor do intend to be, by all that's good;

Cor. By all that's good never.

Gall. So,—and you are reall honeſt, and of quallity?

Cor. Or may *I* ſtill be wretched!

Gall. So, then farewell honeſty and quallity!—S'death what a
night, what hopes, and what a Miſtriſs; have I all loſt for honeſty
and quallity!   [*offers to go.*

Cor. Stay.——

Gall. I will be wreck't firſt,——let go thy hold!   [*in fury.*
——Unleſs thou wouldſt repent.——   [*in a ſoft tone.*

Cor. I cannot of my fixt reſolves for Virtue!
——But if you could but——love me——Honourably——
For I aſſum'd this habit and this dreſs——

Gall. To cheat me of my heart the readyeſt way!
And now like Gaming Rooks, unwilling to give o're till you have
hook't in my laſt ſtake my body too, you couzen me with honeſty,——
oh Damn the dice——I'le have no more on't I, the game's too deep for
me! unleſs you play'd upon the ſquare, Or *I* cou'd cheat like you——
farewell Quallity!——   [*goes out.*

Cor. He's gone, *Phillipa* run and fetch him back;
I have but this ſhort night allow'd for Liberty!
Perhaps to morrow I may be a ſlave?   [*Ex. Phill.*
——Now a my Conſcience there never came good of this troubleſome
virtue——hang't *I* was too ſerious, but a Devil on't he looks ſo Char-
mingly——and was ſo very preſſing I durſt truſt my gay Humour and
good Nature no farther!   [*She walks about, Sir Signal
peeps and then comes out.*

Sir Sig. He's gone!----fo----ha ha ha---- as I hope to breath Madam, you have moft neatly difpatcht him; poor fool----to compare his wit and his perfon to mine.----

Cor. Hah, the Coxcombe here ftill.----

Sir Sig. Well this Countenance of mine never fail'd me yet:

Cor. Ah---- ⸤ *Looking about on him fees his face black*
fqueeks and runs away.

Sir Sig. Ah, Whe what the Deavilo's that for, ----Whe 'tis I, 'tis I m ft *Sereniffimo Signiora!* ⸤Gall. *returns and* Philipa.

Gall. What noife is that, or is't fome new defigne. To fetch me back again?

Sir Sig. How! *Galliard* return'd!

Gall. Hah! what art thou? a fortall or a Devil?

Sir Sig. How! not know me? now might I pafs upon him moft daintily for a Devil, but that I have been beaten out of one Devilfhip already, and dare venture no more Conjurationing.

Gall. Dog, what art thou----not fpeak! Nay then I'le inform my felf, and try if you be flefh and blood. ⸤*Kicks him, he avoids.*

Sir Sig. No matter for all this----'tis better to be kick't then difcovered, for then I fhall be kill'd!---- and I can facrifice a limb or two to my reputation at any time!

Gall. Death, 'tis the fool, the fool for whom I am abus'd and jilted, 'tis fome revenge to difappoint her cunning, and drive the flave before me----Dog! were you her laft referve.---- ⸤*kicks him, he keeps in his cry.*

Sir Sig. Still I fay Mum!

Gall. The Affe will ftill appear through all difguifes, Nor can the Devils fhape fecure the fool---- ⸤*Kicks him he runs out as*
Cor. enters and holds Gall.

Cor. Hold Tyrant----

Gall. Oh Women! Women! fonder in your Appetites Then Beafts; and more unnatural! For they but couple with their kinde, but you Promifcuoufly fhuffle your Brutes together The fop of bufinefs with the lazy Gown-man----the learned Affe with the Illiterate wit. The empty coxcombe with the Pollititian, as Dull and infignificant as he; from the gay fool made more a beaft by fortune to all the loath'd infirmities of Age!
----Farewell----I fcorn to crowd with the dull Herd! Or graze upon the common where they batten---- ⸤*Goes out.*

Fill. I know he loves, by this concern I know it, And will not let him part difatisfy'd! ⸤*Goes out.*

Cor. ----By all that's good I love him more each ⸤*Enter Marcella.* moment, and know he's deftin'd to be mine.----

----What

⌐—What hopes *Marcella,* what i'st we next shall do?

Mar. Fly to our last reserve, come let's haste and dress ! in that disguise we took our flight from *Vitterbo* in,——and somthing——I resolve !

Cor. My soul informs me what !——I ha't ! a project worthy of us both——Which whilst we dress I'le tell thee,——and by which
My dear *Marcella* we will stand or fall,
'Tis our last stake we set ; and have at all.——

ACT V. SCENE I.

Enter Petro, Tickletext, *from the Garden.*

Tick. HAste honest *Barberacho,* before the day discover us to the wicked world, and that more wicked *Galliard* !

Pet. Well Signior, of a bad turn 'twas a good one, that he took you for Sir *Signal* ! the scandal lys at his door now Sir,——so the Ladders fast, you may now mount and away.——

Tick. Very well go your ways, and commend me honest *Barberacho* to the young Gentlewoman ! and let her know as soon as I may be certain to run no hazard in my Reputation, I'le visit her again !

Pet. I'le warrant ye Signior for the future !

Tick. So, now get you gone left we be discover'd !

Pet. Farewell Signior, *a bon viage.* [*Ex.* Pet. Tick. *descends.*

Tick. 'Tis marvellous dark, and I have lost my Lanthorn in the fray ! [*Groping*]——hah!——where abouts am I—hum—what have we here ! ——ah help help help ! [*stumbles at the Well, gets hold of the rope* I shall be drown'd, fire ! *and slides down in the Bucket.* fire, fire, for I have water enough ! Oh for some house,——some street, nay wou'd *Rome* it self were a second time in flames, that my deliverance might be wrought by the necessity for water,——but no human help is nigh—oh. [*Enter Sir* Sig. *as before.*

Sir Sig. Did ever any Knight adventurer, run through so many disasters in one Night ! my worshipful carkass has been cudgel d most plentifully, first bang'd for a coward, which by the way was none of my fault, I cannot help Nature ! then clawd away for a *Diavillo* ! there I was th'e fool ! but who can help that too ! frighted with *Gall's* coming into an Ague, then chimney'd into a Feavor, where I had a fine regale of soot, a perfume which nothing but my *Cacamarda Orangate* cou'd excell ! and which I finde by—[*snufs*] my smelling has defac'd Natures 'mage, and a second time made me be suspected for a devil !—— let me see,—— [*Opens his Lanthorn and looks on his hands.*

'tis

——'tis fo —! am in a clenly pickle! if my face be of the fame peice, I
am fit to fcare away old *Belzebub* himfelfe faith ::   [*Wipes his face.*
——Ay——'tis fo——like to like quoth the devil to the Collier ! well
I'le home, fcrub my felf clean if poffible, get me to bed, devife a handfome lye to excufe my long ftay to my Governor and all's well, and the
man has his Mare again !   [*fhuts his Lanthorn and gropes away, runs a-*
gainft the Well.

—que quefto [*feels gently.*]
make me thankfull 'tis fubftantial wood ! by your leave——
                [*Opens his Lanthorn.*
how ! a Well ! fent by providence that I may wafh my felf, left people fmoke me by the fcent, and beat me anew for ftinking:

    [*fets down his Lanthorn, pulls of his Masking coat, and goes to draw water.*
'Tis a damnable heavy Bucket, now do I fancy I fhall look when I am
wafhing my felf, like the figne of the Labour in vain.

Tick. So my cry is gone forth, and I am delivered by Miracle from
this Dungeon of death and darknefs : this cold Element of deftru-
ction.——

Sir *Sig.* Hah—fure I heard a difmal hollow voice.——
         [*Tick. appears in the Bucket, above the Well.*

Tick. What art thou com'ft in charity.——

Sir *Sig.* Ah *le Diavillo ! le Diavillo ! le Diavillo.*——
         [*Lets go the Bucket, and is running frighted away.*
       Enter Fillamour *and Page, he returns.*

—How a man ! was ever wretched wite fo miferable, the devil at one
hand, and a Roman Night-walker at the other ! which danger fhall I
choofe !——   [*Gets to the door of the houfe.*

Tick. So, I am got up at laft——thanks to my Knight, for I am fure
'twas he ! hah he's here——I'le hear his bufinefs. [*Goes neer to* Fillamour.

Fill. Confound this woman ! this bewitching woman,
I cannot fhake her from my fullen heart,
Spight of my Soul I linger here abouts ;
And cannot to *Vitterbo.*

Tick. Very good ! a dainty Rafcall this !

Enter Galliard *with a Lanthorn, as from* Silvia's *houfe, held by* Philipa.

Fill.—Hah who's this coming from her houfe, perhaps 'tis *Galliard* !
Gall. No Argument fhall fetch me back by Heaven ?
Fill. 'Tis the mad Rogue !

Tick. Oh Lord 'tis *Galliard* ! and angry too, now cou'd I but get off
and leave Sir *Signal* to be beaten, 'twere a rare project,——but 'tis im-
poffible without difcovery.

Fill. But will you hear her Signior !

                            Gall.

Gall. That is, will I lofe more time about her? plague on't I have thrown away already fuch Songs, and fonets, fuch Madrigalls and Tofies, fuch Night walks, fighs, and direfull Lovers looks, as wou'd have mollify'd any woman of Confcience and Religion! and now to be popt 'ith mouth with Quality! well if ever you catch me lying with any but honeft well meaning Damzells hereafter hang me :—farewell old fecret farewell!   [_Ex._ Philipa.

—Now am afham'd of being cuzend fo damnably, _Fillamour_ that virtuous Rafcall will fo laugh at me! s'heart cou'd I but have debaucht him, we had been on equall terms,—but I muft help my felf with lying, and fwear have—a—

Fill. You fhall not need, i'le keep your counfel Sir!

Gall. Hah—_eftevousla!_—

Tick. How _Fillamour_ all this while, fome comfort yet, I am not the only profeffor that diffembles! but how to get away.—

Gall. Oh _Harry_, the moft damnably defeated!   [_A noife of fwords_

Fill. Hold! what noife is that! two men coming this way as from the houfe of the Curtizans.

        [_Enter_ Julio _backwards fighting_ Octavio _and bravo's!_

Gall. Hah on retreating,— sdeath I've no fword!

        Enter Julio _and_ Octavio _fighting._

Fill. Here's one! I'le take my Pages!   [_Takes the Boys fword._
Gall. Now am I mad for mifchief, here hold my Lanthorn Boy!

        [_They fight on_ Julio's _fide, and fight_ Octavio _out at tother fide!_
        Enter Laura _and_ Sabina! _at the fore-door---which is the fame,_
        where Sir Signal _ftands,_ Tick. _groping up that way! finds Sir_
        Sig. _juft entering in:_ Lau. _and_ Sab. _pafs over the ftage._

Sir _Sig._ Hah a door open! I care not who it belongs too, 'tis better dying within doors like a man then in the ftreet like a dog!

        [_Going in_ Tick. _in great fear comes up and pulls him._

Tick. Signior! a gentle Signior, whoe're ye are that owns this Manfion, I befeech you to give protection to a wretched man! half dead with fear and injury!

Sir _Sig._ Nay, I defy the devil to be more dead with fear then I!--Signior you may enter! perhaps 'tis fome body that will make an excufe for us both,—but hark they return!

        [_And both go in: juft after_ Laura _and_ Sabina _enter._

Lau. He's gone! he's gone! perhaps for ever gone,—tell me thou filly manager of Love! how got this Ruffian in, how was it poffible without thy knowledge,—he cou'd get admittance.

Sab. Now as I hope to live and learn I know not Madam! unlefs he follow'd you when you let in the Cavalier, which being by dark he

                    eafily

eafily conceal'd himfelf; no doubt fome Lover of the *Silvianetta's* who miftaking you for her! took him too for a Rival!

Lau. 'Tis likely, and my Fortune is too blame, my curfed Fortune Who like Mifers, deals her fcanty bountys with fo flow a hand, That or we dy before the blessing falls, Or have it fnatcht ere we can call it ours!

[*Raving.*] To have him in my houfe, to have him kinde! Kind as young Lovers when they meet by ftelth : As fond as Age to Beauty! and as foft, As Love and wit cou'd make impatient youth, Preventing even my wifhes and defires, ——Oh Gods! and then! even then to be defeated, Then from my ore joy'd Arms to have him fnatch't; Then when our vows, had made our freedome lawfull! What Maid cou'd fuffer a furprife fo cruel! ——The day begins to break,—go fearch the ftreets, And bring me news he's fafe or I am loft. [*Enter* Gall. Fill. *and* Julio.

Fill. Galliard! where art thou!

Gall. Here fafe and by thy fide.—

Lau. 'Tis he!

Jul. Who ere he were, the Rogue fought like a fury, and but for your timely aid I'de been in fome danger!

Fill. But *Galliard,* thou wert telling me thy adventure with *Silvianetta*! there may be comfort in't.

Lau. So, now I fhall hear with what concern he fpeaks of me.-[*afide.*

Gall. Oh damn her, damn her!

Lau. Hah!

Gall. The very'ft jilt that ever learnt the Art. [*Afide.*

Lau. Heavens!

Gall. Death the whore took me, for fome Amorous Englifh Elder Brother! and was for Matrimony in the devils name! thought me a loving fool, that nere had feen fo glorious a fight before! and wou'd at any rate enjoy!

Lau. Oh Heavens! I am amaz'd! How much he differs from the thing he was, but a few minutes fince. [*Afide.*

Gall. And to advance her price, fet up for Quality! nay fwore fhe was a Maid! and that fhe did but Act the Curtizan!

Lau. Which then he feem'd to give a credit too,——oh the forfworn diffembler.

Gall. But when I came to the matter then in debate, fhe was for Honourable Love forfooth, and wou'd not yield no marry wou'd fhe, not under a Licence from the Parfon of the Parifh.

Jul. Who was it prethee, 'twere a good deed to be fo reveng'd on her!

Gall. Pox on her no, I'me fure fhe's a damn'd gipfie, for at the fame time

time she had her Lovers in reserve, lay hid in her Bed-Chamber.

Lau. 'Twas that he took unkindly.
And makes me guilty of that rude Address!

Fill. Another Lover had she!

Gall. Yes, our Coxcomb Knight *Buffoon,* laid by for a relli?hing b??, in case I prov'd not season'd to her minde.

Lan. Hah! he knew him then!

Gall. But damn her, she passes with the Night, the day will bring new Objects.

Fill. Oh I do not doubt it *Frank!*

Lau. False and inconstant! Oh I shall rave *Silvio.* ——[*Aside to* Silv.

Enter Cornelia! *in Mans Cloathes with a Letter.*

Cor. Here be the Cavaliers! give me kinde Heaven but hold of him, and if I keep him not, I here renounce my charms of wit and Beauty? ——Signiors, is there a Cavalier amongst ye call'd *Fillamour.*

Fill. I own that name; what wou'd you Sir.

Cor. Only deliver this Signior.

[*Fill. goes aside opens his Lanthorn and reads,* Jul. *and* Gall *talk aside.*

Fill. [*Reads.*] I'le only tell you I am Brother to that *Marcella* whom you have injur'd; to oblige you to meet me an hour hence, in the *Piazo Despagnia!* I need not say with your sword in your hand, since you will there meet,——*Julio Sebastiano, Morisini :*——hah! her Brother sure——return'd from Travel,   [*Aside.*

——Signior——I will not fail to answer it as he desires,   [*to* Cornelia.
I'le take this opportunity to steal off undiscover'd,   [*Aside going out.*

Cor. So I've done my sisters business, now for my own.

Gall. But my good friend, pray what adventure have you been on to Night.

Jul. Faith Sir, 'twas like to have prov'd a pleasant one, I came just now from the *Silvianetta,*——the fair young Curtizan.

Cor. Hah! what said the man——came from me!   [*Aside.*

Gall. How Sir, you with *Silvianetta!* when?

Jul. Now, all the dear live long Night.

Cor. A pox take him, who can this be?——   [*Aside.*

Gall. This Night! this Night! that is not yet departed!

Jul. This very happy Night :——I told you I saw a lovely woman at St. *Peters* Church.

Gall. You did so.

Jul. I told you too I follow'd her home, but cou'd learn neither her Name nor quality, but my Page getting ino the acquaintance of one of hers, brought me news of both : her Name *Silvianetta,* her quality a Curtizan!

Cor. I at Church yesterday! Now hang me if I had any such devout thoughts about me, whe what a damn'd scandalous Rascall this.

softly whisper'd me, come to my bofome and be fafe for ever ! and doubtlefs took me for fome happier man.

Lau. Confufion on him, 'twas my very language ! [*Afide raving.*

Jul. Then led me by dark, into her Chamber !

Cor. Oh this damn'd lying Rafcall ! I do this ? [*Afide.*

Jul. But oh the things, the dear obliging things, the kinde the fair young charmer faid and did.

Gall. To thee !

Jul. To me.

Gall. Did *Silvianetta* do this, *Silvianetta* the Curtizan.

Jul. That paffes Sir for fuch, but is indeed of quality.

Cor. This ftranger is the devil ! how fhou'd he know that fecret elfe.

Jul. She told me too 'twas for my fake alone, whom from the firft minute fhe faw, fhe Lov'd ! fhe had affum'd that Name and that dif- guife, the fooner to invite me.

Lau. 'Tis plain, the things I utter'd !——oh my heart !

Gall. Curfe on the publique jilt, the very flattery fhe wou'd have paft on me.

Cor. Pox take him, I muft draw on him, I cannot hold ! [*Afide.*

Gall. Was ever fuch a whore.

Lau. Oh that I knew this man, whom by miftake ! [*Afide.*
I lavifht all the fecrets of my foul too ! [*Afide.*

Jul. I preft for fomething more then dear expreffions,
And found her yield apace,
But fighing told me, of a fatall Contract,
She was oblig'd to make to one fhe never faw,
And yet if I wou'd vow to Marry her, when fhe cou'd prove to
Merrit it, fhe wou'd deny me nothing.

Lau. 'Twas I, by Heaven that heedlefs fool was I.

Jul. Which I with Lovers eager joy perform'd,
And on my knees utter'd the hafty words,
Which fhe repeated ore and gave me back !

Gall. So, he has fwallow'd with a vengeance the very bait fhe had prepar'd for me, or any body that wou'd bite. [*Afide.*

Jul. But ere I cou'd receive the dear reward of all my vows,
I was drawn upon, by a man that lay hid in her Chamber :
Whether by chance or defign I know not, who fought me out,
And was the fame you found me engag'd with.

                                                                      Cor.

Cor. A pleasant Rascall this, as ere the devil taught his lesson too.

Gall. So, my comfort is she has jilted him too most damnably.

Cor. 'Slife I have anger enough to make me valiant, why shou'd I not make use on't, and beat this lying Villain whilst the fit holds.

Gall. And you design to keep these vows, though you're contracted to another woman?

Jul. I neither thought of breaking those, or keeping these, My soul was all imploy'd another way.

Lau.——It shall be so,——*Silvio*——I've thought upon a way that must redeem all,——hark and observe me.——

[*Takes* Sil. *and whispers to him.*

Jul. But I'me impatient to pursue my adventure, Which I must endeavour to do, before the light discover the mistake;——Farewell Sir. [*Ex.* Julio.

Gall. Go and be ruin'd quite, she has the knack of doing it.

Silv. I'le warrant ye Madam for my part. [*Ex.* Laura *!*

Gall.——I have a damn'd hankering after this woman, why cou'd not I have put the cheat on her, as *Julio* has, I stand as little on my word as he! a good round Oath or two had done the business,——but a pox on't I lov'd too well to be so wise. [Silvio *comes up to him.*

Sab. Conlicentia Signior *!* Is your name *Galliard*?

Gall. I am the man sweet-heart,——let me behold thee——hah—— Sans Cour's *!* Page.

Sab. A dews of his Lanthorn, what shall I say now? [*Aside.*
——Softly Signior, I am that Page whose chiefest business is to attend my Lords Mistriss Sir.

Cor. His Mistress : whose Mistress, what Mistress ; s'life how that little word has nettled me ! [*Aside listening close.*

Gall. Upon my life the woman that he boasted of. [*Aside hugging*
——a fair young Amorous—Noble——Wanton a—— *himself.*
And she wou'd speak with me my lovely boy?

Sab. You have prevented the commands I had *!* but should my Lord know of it ;——

Gall. Thou wert undone ! I understand thee——
And will be as secret as a Confessor——
As lonely shades, or everlasting Night——come lead the way.——

Cor. Where I will follow thee, though to the bed of her thou'rt going too, and even prevent thy very business there.—— [*Aside.*

Exeunt.

Enter Laura *as before in a Night-gown.* Scene, *A Chamber.*

Lau. Now for a power that never yet was known
To charm this stranger quickly into love,

I 2 *Assist*

Affift my eyes thou God of kinde defires ;
Infpire my language with a moving force
That may at once gain and fecure the Victory. *Enter* Sil.

Sab. Madam your Loyers here : your time's but fhort, confider too :
Count *Julio* may arrive !

Lau. Let him arrive ! having fecur'd my felf of what I love,
I'le leave him to complain his unknown loffe.
To careleffe winds as pittyleff as : : *Sabina* fee the Rooms
Be fill'd with lights ! whilft I prepare my felf to entertain him.
Darknefs fhall ne're deceive me more—— [*Enter to* Sil. Gall.*gazing
about him* Cor. *peeping at the door.*

Gall. All's wonderous rich,——Gay as the Court of love,
But ftill and filent as the fhades of death ;
——Hah——Mufick ! and Excelient ! [*Soft Mufick whilft they fpeak*
Foxon't——but where's the woman——: need no preparation.——

Cor. No you are always provided for fuch incounters and can fall too
Sans Ceremony,——but I may fpoil you ftomack. [*A Song tuning.*

Gall. A voice too, by Heaven and 'tis a fweet one :
Grant fhe be young and I'le excufe the reft.
Yet vie for pleafure with the happyeft Roman !

[*The Song as by* Laura, *after which foft Mufick till fhe enters.*

The SONG By a Perfon of Quality.

FArewell the World and mortal cares
The ravifht Strephon cry'd,
As full of joy and tender tears
He lay by hillis fide :
Let others toyl for wealth and fame,
Whilft not one thought of mine,
At any other blifs fhall aim,
But thofe dear arms, but thofe dear arms of thine.

Still let me gaze on thy bright eyes,
And hear thy charming tongue,
I nothing ask, increafe my joys
But thus to feel 'em long ;
In clofe embraces let us lye,
And fpend our lives to come,
Then let us both together dye
And be each others, be each others Tomb.

——Death

—Death I am fir'd already with her voice.—

Cor. So, I am like to thrive,—   [*Enter* Julio.

Jul. What mean these lights in every room, as if to make the day without the Sun : and quite destroy my hopes !—hah *Galliard* here !

Cor. A man ! grant it some Lover, or some Husband Heaven !
Or any thing that will but spoil the sport,
The Lady ! oh blast her ! how fair she is.

     [*Enter* Laura *with her Lute drest in a careless rich dress, follow'd by*
       Sabina *to whom she gives her Lute.*

Jul. Hah ! 'tis the same woman !   [*Sees* Julio *and starts.*

Lau. A stranger here ! what Art can help me now.—   [*She pauses.*

Gall. By all my joys a lovely woman 'tis,

Lau. Help me deceipt, dissembling, all that's woman—.
         [*She starts and gazes on* Gall. *pulling* Silvio.

Cor. Sure I shou'd know that face.—

Lau. Ah look my *Silvio* ! is't not he !—it is !
That smile, that Air, that meen, that Bow is his !
'Tis he by all my hopes, by all my wishes !

Gall. He, yes yes, I am a He, I thank my stars !
And never blest 'em half so much for being so,
As for the dear variety of woman !

Cor. Curse on her charms shee'l make him love in earnest.

Lau. It is my Brother ! and report was false !   [*Going towards him.*

Gall. How her Brother ! Gad I'me sorry we're so neer akin with all
My soul ; for I am damnably pleas'd with her !

Lau. Ah why do ye shun my Arms —or are ye Ayr !
And not to be inclos'd in human twines—
Perhaps you are the Ghost of that dead Lord !
That comes to whisper vengance to my soul.

Lau. Shart ! a Ghost ! this is an odd preparative to love,   (*Aside.*

Cor. 'Tis *Laura* ! my Brother *Julio's* Mistress, and Sister to *Octavio* !

Gall. Death, Madam, do not scare away my love, with tales of
Ghosts, and fancies of the dead, I'le give ye proofs I'me living loving man, as errant an Amorous a Mortall as heart can wish — I hope
she will not jilt me too.   [*Aside.*

Cor. So he's at his common proof for all Arguments
If she shou'd take him at his word now, and she'l be sure to do't.

Lau. Amiable stranger pardon the mistake !
And charge it on my passion for a Brother !
Devotion was not more retir'd then I,
Vestals, or widow'd Matrons when they weep,
Till by a fatall chance I saw in you ;
The dear resemblance of a Murther'd Brother !   [*Weeps.*

                           Jul.

Jul. What the devil can she mean by this.   [*Aside.*

Lau. I durst not trust my eyes, yet still I gaz'd,
And that encreas'd my faith you were my Brother,
But since they err'd, and he indeed is dead,
Oh give me leave to pay you all that love,
That tenderness and passion that was his!   [*Weeping.*

Cor. So, I knew she wou'd bring matters about some way or other,
oh mischief mischief help me ! 'slife I can be wicked enough when I
have no use on't, and now I have, I'me as harmless as a fool.

        [*As* Gall. *is earnestly talking to* Lau. Julio *pulls him by the sleeve.*

Lau. Oh save me ! save me from the Murderer !
Jul. Hah !
Gall. A Murderer where !
Lau. I faint, I dye with horror of the sight.
Gall. Hah——my friend a Murderer ! sure you mistake him Madam,
he saw not *Rome* till yesterday,—an honest youth Madam and one that
knows his distance upon occasion !—'slife how cam'st thou here——
prethee begone and leave us !

Jul. Why do you know this Lady Sir.
Gall. Know her !—a——ay ay——man——and all her Relations, she's
of quality,—withdraw withdraw——Madam——a—he is my friend
and shall be civil.——

Lau. I have an easie faith for all you say,——but yet however innocent he be or dear to you, I beg he wou'd depart——he is so like my
brothers Murtherer, that one look more wou'd kill me——

Jul. A Murtherer ! charge me with cowardise, with Rapes or Trea-
sons—Gods a Murtherer!

Cor. A devil on her ! she has rob'd the sex of all their arts of cunning.

Gall. Pox on't thou'rt rude ! go, in good manners go——
Lau. I do conjure ye torture me no more,
If you wou'd have me think you're not that Murtherer.
Be gone——and leave your Friend to calm my heart
Into some kinder thoughts !

Gall. Ay, ay, prithee go ! I'le be sure to do thy business for thee ;
Cor. Yes, yes, you will not fail to do a friendly part no doubt——
Jul. 'Tis but in vain to stay——I see she did mistake her man
last Night, and 'twas to chance I am in debt for that good fortune !——
I will retire to show my obedience Madam !

        [*Ex.* Jul. Gall. *going to the door with him.*

Lau. He's gone and left me Mistress of my wish !
Descend ye little winged Gods of Love,
Descend and hover round our bower of blisse,
Play all in various forms about the youth,   [*Aside.*
And

And empty all our quivers at his heart:

[Gall. returns, she takes him by the hand.

——Advance thou dearer to my foul then kindred,
Thou more then Friend or Brother,
Let meaner Souls born bafe conceal the God!
Love owns his Monarchy within my heart,
So Kings that daign to vifit humble roofs :
Enter difguis'd, but in a Noble Palace,
Own their great Power, and fhow themfelves in glory.

Gall. I am all tranfport with this fudain blifs,
And want fome kinde allay to fit my Soul for recompence.

Cor. Yes, yes, my forward friend you fhall have an allay, if all my
Art can do't, to damp thee even to difappointment.

Gall. My Souls all wonder now, let us retire,
And gaze till I have foftend it to Love. *[Going out is met by Cor.*

Cor. Madam !

Lau. More interruption !——hah.—— *[Turns.*

Cor. My Mafter the young *Count Julio.*

Lau. Julio !

Gall. What of him. *[Afide.*

Cor. Being juft now arriv'd at *Rome !*

Lau. Heavens ! arriv'd! *[Afide.*

Cor. Sent me to beg the Honour of waiting on you.

Lau. Sure ftranger you miftake !——

Cor. If Madam you are *Laura Lucretia !*——

Gall. *Laura Lucretia !* by Heaven the very woman he's to marry.

[Afide.

Lau. This wou'd furprife a Virgin lefs refolv'd,
But what have I to do with ought but Love ! *[Afide.*
——And can your Lord imagine this an hour,
To make a ceremonious vifit in !

Gall. Ridles by Love ! or is't fome trick again. *[Afide.*

Cor. Madam, where vows are paft, the want of ceremony may be
pardon'd !

Lau. I do not ufe to have my will difputed,
Begone and let him know I'le be obey'd !

Cor. 'Slife fhe'l out-wit me yet,—— *[Afide.*
Madam I fee this nicenefs is not general,
——You can except fome Lovers.

Gall. My pert young confident depart, and let your Mafter know
He'l finde a better welcome from the fair vain Curtizan, *la Silvianetta !*
where he has paft the Night and given his vows.

Lau. Dearly devis'd and I muft take the hint. *[Afide fmiling.*

Cor. He knows me fure, and fays all this to plague me. *[Afide.*
My Lord, my Mafter with a Curtizan ! he's but juft now ariv'd

Gall. A pretty focward fawcy lying boy this! and may do well in time,——Madam believe him not, I faw his Mafter yefterday,——converft with him,——' know him he's my friend!—'twas he that parted hence but now,——he told me all his paffion for a Curtizan, fcarce half an hour fince.

Cor. So!

Lau. I do not doubt it, oh how I love him for this feafonable lye, ——And can you think i'le fee a perjur'd man,   [*To* Cor.
Who gives my intreft in him to another,
——Do i not help ye out moft Artfully.——   [*And laughing to* Gall.

Cor. I fee they are refolv'd to out face me.

Gall. Nay vow'd to marry her!

Lau. Heavens to marry her!

Cor. To be conquer'd at my own weapon too,—lying 'tis a hard cafe!——   [*Afide.*

Gall. Go boy you may be gone, you have your Anfwer childe,
And may depart——come Madam let us leave him.

Cor. Gone! no help, death I'le quarrel with him,——nay fight him, —Damn him,——rather then loofe him thus,—ftay Signior,[*I ulls him.*
——You call me boy,——but you may finde your felf miftaken Sir,——
And know—I've that about me may convince ye,   [*Showing his fword.*
—'T has done fome Execution!

Gall. Prethee on whom or what? fmall Village curs!
The barking of a Maftive wou'd unman thee.   [*Offers to go.*

Cor. Hold——follow me from the refuge of her Arms!
As thou'rt a man, I do conjure thee do't:
——' hope he will, I'le venture beating for't.   [*Afide.*

Gall. Yes, my brisk——little Rafcal——I will——a——

Lau. By all that's good you fhall not ftir from hence, ho who waits there, *Antonio, Silvio, Gafpero,* [*Enter all*]—take that firce youth and bear him from my fight.

Cor. You fhall not need, 'slife thefe rough Rogues will be too hard for me,——'ve one prevention left;——farewell,
Maift thou fupply her with as feable Art,
As I fhou'd do, were I to play thy part.   [*Goes out with the reft.*

Gall. He's gone! Now lets redeem our bleffed minutes loft. [*Goin*
    Scene changes to the Street.——   Piazo Defpagnia!
       Enter Julio *alone.*

Jul. Now by this breaking daylight I cou'd rave, I knew fhe miftook me laft Night which made me fo eager to improve my luckey minutes,——fure *Galliard* is not the man, I long to know the miftery, ——hah——who's here—*Fillamour.*

   [*Enter* Fillamour *met by* Marcella *in Mans Clothes, they pafs by*
    each other——cock and juftle.

Mar. I take it——you are he I look for Sir!

                 Fill.

Fill. My Name is *Fillamour.*

Mar. Mine,——*Julio Sebaſtiano Muriſini.*

Jul. Hah, my Name by Heaven.　　　　　　　　　　[*Aſide.*

Fill. I doubt it not, ſince in that Lovely face,
I ſee the charming Image of *Marcella* !

Jul. Hah.——

Mar. You might, ere Travel rufled me to man,
——I ſhou'd return thy praiſe whilſt I ſurvey thee,
But that I came not here for Complement,——draw.——　　[*Draws.*

Fill. Why cauſe thou'rt like *Marcella?*

Mar. That were ſufficient reaſon for thy hate,
But mine's becauſe thou baſt betray'd her baſely;
——She told me all the ſtory of her Love,
How well you meant, how honeſtly you ſwore,
And with a thouſand tears imploy'd my Aid :
·To break the contract ſhe was forc't to make,
T' *Octavio,* and give her to your Arms.
I did, and brought you word of our deſign,
——I need not tell ye what returns you made ;
Let it ſuffice my Siſter was neglected,
Neglected for a Curtizan,——a whore !
I watcht and ſaw each circumſtance of falſhood,

Jul, Damnation ! what means this?

Fill. I ſcorn to ſave my life by lyes or flatterys,
But credit me, the Viſit that I made,
I durſt have ſworn had been to my *Marcella* !
Her Face, her Eyes, her Beauty was the ſame,
Only the buſineſs of her Language differ'd,
And undeceiv'd my hope.

Mar. In vain thou think'ſt to flatter me to faith,——
When thou'dſt my Siſters Letter in thy hand, which ended that diſpute
Even then I ſaw with what regret you read it :
What care you took to diſobey it too,——
The ſhivering Maid, half dead with fears and terrors of the Night,
In vain expected a relief from Love or thee,
Draw that I may return her the glad news I have reveng'd her.

Jul. Hold much miſtaken youth ! 'tis I am *Julio,* thou *Fillamour* know'ſt
my Name, knows I ariv'd but yeſterday at *Rome,* and heard the killing
news of both my Siſters flights, *Marcella* and *Cornelia,*——and thou art
ſome Impoſture.　　　　　　　　　　　　　　　　　[*To* Marcella.

Mar. If this now ſhou'd be true, I were in a fine condition.——

Fill. Fled ! *Marcella* fled !

Jul. 'Twas ſhe I told thee yeſterday was loſt,
But why art thou concern'd,——explain the Miſtery !

Fill. I lov'd her more then life ! nay even than Heaven !

　　　　　　　　　　　　　K　　　　　　　　　　　　And

And doſt thou queſtion my concern for her,
Say how! a▵d why! and whether is ſhe fled!

Jul. Oh wou'd I knew, that I might kill her in **her Lovers Arms,**
Or if I found her innocent, reſtore her to *Octavio!*

Fill. To *Octavio!* and is my friendſhip of ſo little worth,
You cannot think I merrit her.

Jul. This is ſome trick between 'em! but I have ſworn moſt ſolemnly, have ſworn by Heaven and my Honour to reſign her, and I will
do't or dye,——therefore declare quickly, declare where ſhe's, or I will
leave thee dead upon the place.   [*To* Marcella.

Mar. So, death or *Octavio,* a pretty hopefull choice this.

Fill. Hold! by Heaven you ſhall not touch a ſingle hair, thus——
will I guard the ſecret in his boſome.   [*Puts himſelf between 'em draws.*

Jul. 'Tis plain thouſt injur'd me,——and to my Honour I'le ſacrifice
my friendſhip, follow me.   [*Enter* Petro *and* Cornelia.

Mar. Ah *Petro,* fly fly ſwift and reſcue him.——[*Exiunt* Pet. *with his*

Cor. Oh have *I* found thee, fit for my purpoſe too. *ſword in his hand.*
Come haſt along with me,——thou muſt preſent my Brother *Julio* in
ſtantly, or I am loſt, and my projects loſt, and my mans loſt, and all's
loſt.   *Enter* Petro.

Pet. *Victoria, Victoria,* your Cavaliers and Conqueror! the other
wounded in his ſword hand, was eaſily diſarm'd.

Mar. Then lets retire, if I am ſeen I'me loſt,——*Petro* ſtay here for
the Cavalier, and conduct him to me to this houſe;——I muſt be ſpeedy
now.——

Cor. Remember this is *Julio!*   [*Pointing to* Marcella!

Pet. I know your deſign and warrant ye my part:——hah *Octavio.*
          Enter Octavio, Muriſini, *and* Crapine.

Oct. Now cowardiſe that everlaſting infamy, dwel' ever on my face,
that men may point me out that hated Lover, that ſaw his Miſtreſs
falſe, ſtood tamely by whilſt ſhe repeated vows! nay was ſo infamous
ſo dully tame, to hear her ſwear her hatred and averſion, yet ſtill I
calmly liſtend! thongh my ſword were ready, and did not cut his
throat for't.

Mur. I thought, you'd ſaid you'd fought.

Oct. Yes, I did rouſe at laſt and wak'd my wrongs,
But like an Aſs a patient fool of Honour,
I gave him friendly Notice I wou'd kill him;
And fought like prizers not as angry Rivals.

Mur. Why that was hanſome,——I love fair play what wou'd you
elſe have done!

Oct. Have fall'n upon him like a ſudain ſtorm, [*Enter* Pet. *and* Fill.
quick unexpected in his height of Love:——ſee——ſee yonder! or I'me
miſtaken by this glimering day or that is *Fillamour;* now entering at
her door, 'tis he by my revenge!——what ſay you Sir!

                                        Mur.

Mur. By th' Mafs I think it was he,——*Enter* Julio.

Oct. Julio I've caught the wantons in their toyl,
I have 'em faft, thy fifter and her Lover.   [*Embraces him.*

Jul. Eternal fhame light on me, if they fcape then *!*

Oct. Follow me quick,——whilft we can get admittance.

Jul. Where——here *!*

Oct. Here,—come all and fee her fhame and my Revenge.

Jul. And are you not miftaken in the houfe.

Oct. Miftaken ! *I* faw the Ravifher enter juft now, thy Uncle faw it
too, oh my Exceffive joy, come if *I* lye—fay *I*'me a dog a Villain !
                                                       [*Exeunt as into the Houfe.*

Scene changes to a Chamber, Enter Sir Signal—*a little groping.*

Sir Sig. There's no finding my way out,—and now does fear make
me fancy,——this fome *I*nchanted Caftle.——   [*Enter* Tick. *liftening.*

Tick. Hah an *I*nchanted Caftle !

Sir Sig. Belonging to a monfterous Giant ! who having fpirited a-
way the King of *Tropicipopicans* Daughter, keeps her here inclos'd, and
that *I* wandering Knight am by fickle Fortune fent to her deliverance.
                                                       [Tick. *liftens.*

Tick. How's that ! fpirited away the King of *Tropicipopicans* daughter ! blefs me what unlawfull wickednefs is practic'd, in this Romifh
Heathenifh Countreys !   [*Afide.*

Sir Sig. And yet the devil of any dwarfe Squire or Damzel have *I*
met with yet :——wou'd *I* were clenlily off a this bufinefs,——hah lights
as *I* live *!* and people coming this way *!*——blefs me from the Giant,——
Oh Lord what fhall *I* do.——   [*Falls on his knees.*

Tick. *I* fear no Giants, having juftice on my fide, but Reputation
makes me tender of my perfon !——hah——what's this a Curtain : *I*'le
winde my felf in this, it may fecure me !
                                                       [*Winds himfelf in a window Curtain.*

Sir Sig.——They're entering, what fhall *I* do——hah——here's a corner ! defend me from a Chimney.

    [*Creeps to the corner of the Window, and feels a fpace between* Tick.
    legs and the corner, creeps in and ftands up juft behind Tickletext.
    Enter Gall. *leading* Laura *!* Sab. *with lights juft after 'em !* Jul.
    Oct. Mur. *and* Crap.

Oct. Juft in the happy minute.

Gall. *I*'ve fworn by every God *!* by every power divine ! to Marry
thee ! and fave thee from the Tyranny of a forc't Contract,—Nay Gad
if *I* loofe a fine wench for want of Oaths this bout the devil's in me.

Oct. What think ye now Sir.

Jul. Damnation on her, fet my rage at liberty !   [Mur. *holds him.*
that *I* may kill 'em both !

Mur. *I* fee no caufe for that, fhe may be virtuous yet.

Oct. De ye think as fuch to pafs her off on me,

Or that I'le bear the infamy of your Family,

No I scorn her now, but can revenge my Honour on a Rival!

Mur. Nay then I'le see fair play,—turn and defend thy life. [*goes to*

Jul. Whilſt I do juſtice on the Proſtitute! —hah—— *Gall. who turns.*

Defend me 'tis the woman that I Love.   [*He gazes! ſhe runs to* Gall.

Lau. Octavio!

Oct. Laura! my ſiſter! perfidious ſhamefull!—— [*Offers to kill her.*

Jul. Hold! thy ſiſter this? that ſiſter I'me to marry!   (wretched.

Lau. Is this then *Julio!* and do all the powers conſpire to make me

Oct. May I be dumb for ever!

    [*Holds his ſword down and looks ſadly,* Jul. *holds* Lau. *by one hand*

          pleads with Oct. *with the other, Enter* Fillamour *and* Pet.

Fill.——Hah *Galliard!* in danger too!   [*Draws.*

                    [*ſteps to 'em!* Mur. *puts between.*

Oct. Fillamour here, how now what's the matter friend.

                  [*they talk whilſt Enter* Marcella *and* Cornelia.

Cor. Hah new broyls, ſure the devil's broke looſe to Night!——my

Uncle as I live!   [Mur. *pleads between.* Fill. *and* Octavio.

Mar. And *Octavio!* where ſhall we fly for ſafety!

Cor. I'le ene truſt to my Breeches! 'tis too late to retreat!——'slife

here be our Cavaliers too, nay then nere fear falling into the Enemies

hands!

Fill. I, I fled with *Marcella!* had I been bleſt with ſo much Love

from her, I wou'd have boaſted on't 'ith face of Heaven.

Mur. La ye Sir.   [*To* Octavio!

Fill. The lovely Maid, I own I have a paſſion for;

But by the powers above the flame was ſacred,

And wou'd no more have paſt the bounds of Honour,

Or hoſpitallity! then I wou'd baſely Murther! and were ſhe free,

I wou'd from all the World make her for ever mine.

Mur. Look ye Sir, a plain caſe this.

Gall. He tells ye ſimple truth Sir.

Oct. Was it not you, this ſcarce paſt Night I fought with here, in

the houſe by dark! juſt when you had exchanged your vows with her!

Lau. Heavens! was it he?   [*Aſide.*

Fill. This minute was the firſt I ever entred here!

Jul. 'Twas I Sir, was that interrupted Lover,—and this the Lady!

Lau. And muſt I yield at laſt.   [*Aſide.*

Oct. Wonders and Ridles!

Gall. And was this the *Silvianetta* Sir, you told the ſtory of! [*ſlyly.*

Jul. The ſame whom inclination, friends and deſtiny,

Conſpire to make me bleſt with.

Gall. So many diſappointments in one Night, wou'd make a man

turn honeſt in ſpight of Nature!   [*Sir* Sig. *peeps from behind.*

Sir Sig. Some comfort yet, that I am not the only fool defeated!

hah! *Galliard.*   *Oct.*

Oct. I'me satisfied! [*to* Fill.]——but what cou'd move you Sir, —— [*to* Gall.] to injure me! one of my Birth and Quality!

Gall. Faith Sir I never stand upon ceremony when there's a woman in the case,——nor knew I 'twas your Sister: Or if I had I shou'd alik'd her nere the worse for that, had she been kind.

Jul. It is my business to account with him, And I am satisfy'd he has not injur'd me! he is my friend!

Gall. That's frankly said! and uncompel'd I swear she's innocent!

Oct. If you're convinc't! I too am satisfy'd! And give her to you whilst that faith continues!   [*Gives him her.*

Lau. And must I, must I force my heart to yield! [*Aside.* And yet his generous confidence Obliges me!   [*Aside.*

Oct. And here I vow! by all the sacred Powers, [*Kneels.*] that punish perjury, never to set my heart on faithless woman!——Never to Love nor Marry! [*Rises.*] Travel shall be my business,——thou my Heir!   [*To Jul.o.*

Sir Sig. So, poor soul, I warrant he has been defeated too!

Mar. Marcella Sir will take ye at your word!

Fill. Marcella!

Mar. Who owns with blushes truths shou'd be conceal'd, but to prevent more mischief,——that I was yours Sir was against my will, [*to* Oct. my soul was *Fillamours* ere you claim'd a right in me; though I nere saw or held discourse with him, but at an awful distance,——nor knew he of my flight.

Oct. I do believe, and give thee back my claim, I scorn the brutal part of Love! the noblest body where the heart is wanting.

[*They all talk aside,* Cornelia *comes up to* Galliard!

Cor. Whe how now Cavalier! how like a discarded favorite do you look now, who whilst your Authority lasted laid about ye; domineerd huft and blusterd, as if there had been no end on't, now a man may approach ye without terror!——you see the meats snatcht out of your mouth Sir, the Lady's dispos'd on! who's Friends and Relations you were so well acquainted with.

Gall. Peace boy, I shall be angry else.——

Cor. Have you never a cast Mistress that will take compassion on you: faith what think you of the little Curtizan now!

Gall. As ill as ere I did! what's that to thee.

Cor. Much more then you're aware on Sir,——and faith to tell you truth I'me no servant to Count *Julio*! but ene a little mischievous instrument she sent hither to prevent your making Love to *Dona Laura*!

Gall. 'Tis she her self,——how cou'd that beauty hide it self so long from being known! [*Aside.*] —— Malicious little dog in a Manger, that wou'd neither eat, nor suffer the hungry to feed themselves! what spitefull devil cou'd move thee to treat a Lover thus! but I am pretty well reveng'd on ye!

Cor. On me!   *Gall.*

Gall. You think! did not know thofe pretty Eyes! that lovely Mouth I have fo often kift in cold imagination!

Cor. Softly tormentor!   [*They talk afide.*

Mar. In this difgufe we parted from *Vitterbo*! atended only by *Petro*, and *Philipa*! at *Rome* we took the Title and habit of two Curtizans; both to fhelter us from knowledge, and to Oblige *Fillamour* to vifit us, which we beliv'd he wou'd in curiofity, and yefterday it fo fell out as we defir'd!

Fill. How ere my eyes might be impos'd upon, you fee my heart was firm to its firft object, can you forget and pardon the miftake!

Jul. She fhall! and with *Octavio's*—and my Uncles leave,——thus make your Title good.——   [*Gives her to* Fill.

Oct. 'Tis vain to ftrive with deftiny!   [*Gives her.*

Mur. With all my heart,——but where's *Cornelia* all this while!

Gall. Here's the fair ftragler Sir.

    [*Leads her to* Mur. *he holds his Cane up at her.*

Mur. Why thou baggage, thou wicked contriver of mifchief, what excufe hadft thou for running away, thou hadft no Lover?

Cor. 'Twas therefore Sir I went to finde one! and if I am not miftaken in the mark, 'tis this Cavalier I pitch upon for that ufe and purpofe.

Gall. Gad I thank ye for that,——I hope you'l ask my leave firft, I'me finely drawn in efaith!——have *I* been dreaming all this Night, of the poffeffion of a new gotten Miftrefs, to wake and finde my felf nooz'd to a dull wife in the morning.

Fill. Thou talkft like a man that never knew the pleafures thou difpifeft; faith try it *Frank*, and thou wilt hate thy paft loofe way of living.

Cor. And to encourage a young fetter up, I do here promife to be the moft Miftrifs like wife,——you know Signior I have learnt the trade, though I had not ftock to practice, and will be as expenfive, Infolent, vain Extravagant, and Inconftant, as if you only had the keeping part, and another the Amorous Afignations, what think ye Sir.

Fill. Faith fhe pleads well! and ought to cary the caufe!

Gall. She fpeaks Reafon! and I'me refolv'd to truft good Nature! —give me thy dear hand.——   [*They all joyn to give it him, he kiffes it.*

Mur. And now you are both fpeed, pray give me leave to ask ye a civil queftion! are you fure you have been honeft, if you have I know not by what Miracle you have liv'd.

Pet. Oh Sir as for that, I had a fmall ftock of cafh, in the hands of a cuple of Englifh Bankers, on Sir *Signal Buffoon*.——

Sir Sig. Sir *Signal Buffoon*! what a pox does he mean me trow.

                                        [*Peeping.*

Pet.——And one Mr. *Tickletext*!

Tick. How was that,——certo my Name!

    [*Peeps out and both fee each other their faces, being clofe together one at one fide the Curtain, and tother at tother.*

Gall. and *Fill.* Ha ha ha!   •   *Sir Sig.*

Sir Sig. And have I caught you efaith Mr. Governor !
Nay nere put in your head for the matter, here's none but friends mun !

Gall. How now what have we here !

Sir Sig. Speak of the devil and he appears !

[*Pulls his Governor forward.*

Tick. I am nndone !—but good *Sir Signal* do not cry whore first ! as
the old proverb fays !

Sir Sig. And good Mr. Governor, as another old proverb fays, do
not let the kettle call the Pot black-ars !——

Fill. How came you hither Gentlemen !

Sir Sig. Whe ! faith Sir divining of a wedding or two forward, I
brought Mr. Chaplain to give you a caft of his Office, as the faying is.

Fill. What without Book Mr. *Ticklctext.*

Cor. How now ! fure you miftake, thefe are two Lovers of mine.

Sir Sig. How Sir your Lovers! we are none of thofe Sir, we are Eng-
lifhmen !

Gall. You miftake Sir *Signal,* this is *Silvianetta !*

Sir Sir. and *Tick.* How !

[*Afide.*

Gall. Here's another fpark of your acquaintance,--do you know him.

Tick. How *Barberacho !* nay then all will out. ——

Gall. Yes, and your fencing and Civility-Mafter.

Sir Sig. Ay,—whe what was it you that pickt our pockets then,——
and cheated us !

Gall. Moft damnably,——but fince 'twas for the fupply of two fair
Ladys, all fhall be reftor'd again.

Tick. Some comfort that.

Fill. Come lets in and forgive all, 'twas but one Nights Intrigue, in
which all were a little faulty !

Sir Sig. And Governor, pray let me have no more dominering and
Ufurpation ! But as we have hitherto been honeft Brothers in iniquity,
fo let's wink hereafter at each others frailties !

Since Love and women eafily betray man,
From the grave Gown-man to the bufy Lay-man.

The EPILOGUE,

Spoken by Mr. *Smith*.

SO hard the Times are, and so thin the Town,
Though but one Playhouse, that must too lie down;
And when we fail what will the Poets do?
They live by us as we are kept by you:
When we disband, they no more Plays will write,
But make Lampoons, and Libell ye in spight;
Discover each false heart that lies within,
Nor Man nor Woman shall in private sin;
The precise whoring Husbands haunts betray,
Which the demurer Lady to repay,
In his own coin does the just debt defray.
The brisk young Beauty linkt to Lands and Age,
Shuns the dull property, and strokes the youthfull Page;
And if the stripling apprehend not soon,
Turns him aside and takes the brawny Groom,
Vhilst the kinde man so true a Husband proves,
To think all's well done by the thing he loves;
Knows he's a Cuckold, yet content to bear
What 'ere Heaven sends, or horns or lusty heir;
Fops of all sorts he draws more artfully,
Then ever on the Stage did Nokes or Leigh:
And Heaven be prais'd when these are scarce, each Broth
)'th pen, contrive to set on one another:
  These are the effects of angry Poets rage,
Driven from their Winter-Quarters on the Stage,
And when we go, our Women vanish too,
Vhat will the well-fledg'd keeping Gallant do?
And where but here can he expect to finde,
A gay young Dam'sell manag'd to his minde,
Vho ruines him and yet seems wondrous kinde.
)ne insolent and false, and what is worse,
Governs his heart and manages his purse;
Makes him whate're she'd have him to believe,
Spends his Estate, then learns him how to live;
I hope these weighty considerations will
Move ye to keep us all together still;
To treat us equal to our great desert,
And pay your Tributes with a franker heart,
If not, th'aforesaid Ills will come, and we must part.

FINIS.